The Perfect Life

Other Novels By Robin Lee Hatcher

The Perfect Life

A NOVEL

ROBIN LEE HATCHER

THOMAS NELSON
Since 1798

NASHVILLE   DALLAS   MEXICO CITY   RIO DE JANEIRO   BEIJING

Published in Nashville, Tennessee, by Thomas Nelson. Thomas Nelson is a trademark of Thomas Nelson, Inc.

Thomas Nelson, Inc. titles may be purchased in bulk for educational, business, fund-raising, or sales promotional use. For information, please e-mail SpecialMarkets@ThomasNelson.com.

Scripture references are taken from The Contemporary English Version, © 1991 by the American Bible Society. Used by permission. Scripture references are also taken from the Holy Bible, New Living Translation, © 1996. Used by permission of Tyndale House Publishers, Inc., Wheaton, Illinois 60189. All rights reserved.

Publisher's Note: This novel is a work of fiction. Names, characters, places, and incidents are either products of the author's imagination or used fictitiously. All characters are fictional, and any simi-larity to people living or dead is purely coincidental.

Library of Congress Cataloging in Publication Data

Hatcher, Robin Lee.
    The perfect life : a novel / Robin Lee Hatcher.
       p. cm.
       ISBN 978-1-59554-148-2
    1. Married people—Fiction. 2. Scandals—Fiction. 3. Life change events—Fiction. I. Title.
PS3558.A73574P44 2008
813'.54—dc22   2007049263

Printed in the United States of America

08 09 10 11 12 RRD 7 6 5 4

To the wonderful women who meet to plot, play, and pray each summer in the mountains of northern Idaho. Thanks for your friendship, dear sisters, as well as your laughter and abundance of ideas. I treasure each and every one of you.

Whatever is good and perfect comes to us from God above, who created all heaven's lights.

Unlike them, he never changes or casts shifting shadows.

—JAMES 1:17

Part One

PERFECT LIFE

One

⁓

BY TRADITION, SATURDAY MORNINGS WERE SAVORED IN the Clarkson household. My husband, Brad, usually prepared breakfast, and then the two of us—still clad in our pajamas—read snippets from the newspaper to each other while we dined on French toast or omelets or a hash-brown casserole.

On this particular Saturday morning in April, I'd just taken a sip of freshly squeezed orange juice when I picked up the local section of the paper. I opened the fold, saw the headline, and choked.

"Katherine?" Brad rose and came to my aid.

"I'm all right." I waved at him to sit down again, then wiped tears from my eyes. "But look at this."

I laid the paper on the table and turned it toward him, pointing at the headline on the front page.

BRAD CLARKSON: HUMANITARIAN OF THE YEAR
In Step Foundation leader says it truly is more blessed to give

Brad groaned. "Well, if that doesn't make me sound like a prig, I don't know what would."

"But you *did* say it." I tried to hide my amusement. Not very hard, I admit, but I did try. "You told me so."

"Some help you are."

Smiling now, I stood and rounded the table to stand behind Brad so we could read the article together.

There were two photos accompanying the article. The first was of Brad and four of the administrative assistants who worked in the foundation's downtown office. Brad was in the center, his arms around the shoulders of the women on either side of him. All of them were laughing at something. More than likely at something he'd said. The second photo was also of Brad, this time wearing a hard hat, smiling his irresistible smile, and standing in front of one of In Step's finished remodels. Beside him was a petite woman who looked to be in her early thirties. She held a small child in her arms. I could tell there were tears in her eyes as Brad handed her the keys to her new home.

Brad had been in the spotlight often in recent years. He

claimed it made him uncomfortable, that he wished articles and news reports would focus on what the Lord was doing with the ministry, but I wasn't completely convinced. He was a natural with the media, and they loved him. He had an easy charm that drew people to him.

"I wish you'd been with me for that interview," he said.

He often said things like that, but he'd given up asking me a long time ago. He knew it was useless. It had been ten years since I'd been involved with the day-to-day running of the foundation; I wouldn't have anything of interest to say to a reporter. My main role for the last decade—by my own choice—had been as chauffeur for two active teenagers involved in an array of extracurricular activities, as chief cook and bottle washer for my hungry family and many of their friends, and later as mother of the bride at our daughters' weddings.

"You're so beautiful," Brad continued. "If you were in that photo, no one would notice the stupid headline."

Okay, that was one of the reasons I loved Brad so much. He was never short on compliments. He always knew the right words to make me feel good.

I was a woman blessed with a wonderful life. We worked hard and tried to follow Christ as He would have us. And God had blessed us. I couldn't want for anything more than what I had— a wonderful husband, two beautiful daughters, and a couple of grandbabies on the way.

Brad read aloud. "'Clarkson says he never imagined In Step would be anything more than a small charity he and his wife ran out of their home. Seventeen years later, the foundation has provided remodeled, affordable homes for nearly a hundred "recipient families"—as their clients are called—and In Step now occupies an entire floor of the Henderson Building in downtown Boise, employing a staff of twenty-five.'"

"See." I kissed the top of his head. "It's a good article. It will bring much deserved attention to the foundation."

Pride welled in my heart. *Humanitarian of the Year.* No one deserved the accolades more than Brad. In the seventeen years since he was first inspired to create In Step, he'd worked hard to bring his vision to fruition. And God had honored his desire to serve, blessing the foundation far beyond anything I'd ever dreamed possible.

I returned to my chair to finish the last of my breakfast. "What are your plans for the day?"

"I thought I might do some yard work." He grinned. "Or maybe we should spend the day in bed watching old movies until it's time to get ready for the banquet.

I laughed again. "Like that's going to happen."

Not that I wouldn't mind doing as he suggested, but I knew my husband. Unless he was sick—a rare occurrence—he wasn't one to be idle for long. Halfway into *Casablanca* or *Raiders of the Lost Ark* or whatever DVD we chose, he would get some idea that pulled him out of bed and into his den where he would scribble away on a yellow pad or enter text into his laptop as fast as he could type.

The telephone rang. I knew without looking at the caller ID that it would be one of our daughters. I answered on the second ring. "Hello?"

"Mom, have you and Dad seen the paper?" It was Emma, our youngest.

"Yes."

"I like that photo of him in front of one of the remodels. Randy Travis in a hard hat."

Brad rolled his eyes, as if he knew what Emma had said. He'd heard it before. Many times. Although he was a fan of country music, he hated people saying he looked like Travis—even though he did. Same square jaw, complete with tiny cleft in his chin, same deep-set eyes, same thin lips, same high forehead, same touch of gray at his temples. Knowing he hated the comparison, the girls and I teased him about it. Unmercifully.

Our bad.

"I'll tell him you said so."

"What time should Jason and I plan to be there tonight?"

"Six-thirty should be early enough. There's an open bar before the banquet. The dinner is at seven." I settled onto a kitchen stool. "How are you feeling?"

"Getting fatter every day. But at least I don't have morning sickness like Hayley."

"Lucky you."

"Don't I know it."

There were no words to describe how excited I was about becoming a grandmother. And to have two grandbabies arriving this summer? Perfection twice over.

The Call Waiting sound beeped in my ear. I checked the ID. It was Hayley.

"That's your sister calling now. Want to hold on?"

"No. Gotta run. I'll see you and Dad tonight. Love you."

"You too. Bye." I clicked over. "Hi, honey."

"Hi, Mom. I take it you've seen the paper."

"Yes. We've seen it."

"Did Dad notice how much he looks like Randy Travis in that picture?"

"That's what Emma said when she called." I stifled a laugh. "Do you want to tell your dad what you think about the photo? He's sitting right here."

Now Brad definitely knew what we were talking about. He shook his head and waved both hands in a back-off motion. "Give Hayley my love. I'm going to take a shower." He rose and left the kitchen.

"Uh-oh. I'll have to apologize for all of us now." Not really. I knew he wasn't upset. We loved to tease in our family. Brad too. In fact, he was the worst of the lot. "Emma said you're still suffering from morning sickness."

"Ugh. It's awful. I thought you said I'd be over it by now."

"No, I said *I* was over it by four months. Some women are sick throughout their pregnancy. The full nine months."

Hayley groaned. "Just shoot me now."

"Keep those saltines on your nightstand." It was poor comfort but the best I could offer. "You're feeling well enough to come tonight, aren't you?"

"Are you kidding? Steve and I wouldn't miss this for the world. I bought a great new dress for the occasion. No one will guess I'm pregnant."

We chatted a few more minutes, making plans to go shopping the following week, then said our good-byes and I hung up the phone.

I remained on the kitchen stool, staring out the window at our backyard—brushed in shades of spring green and the first appearance of colorful flowers—and thought again how wonderful my life was.

Absolutely perfect.

Nicole

NICOLE SCHUBERT STARED AT THE ARTICLE IN THE morning's paper. The colored photographs were grainy, but that didn't obscure Brad Clarkson's rugged handsomeness. Or his smile. She remembered that smile. She'd seen it hundreds of times.

He wasn't as happy as those photographs made him seem. He had troubles just like anybody else. Nicole had seen through the facade of contentment soon after she went to work for him. She'd seen through it and had tried to help.

And Katherine? She was a throwback to another era, no question about it. Miss Goody Two-Shoes sharing her favorite Bible verses and baking her fancy desserts.

Nicole drew in a deep breath through her nose, trying to quiet the anger curling in her belly. *Humanitarian of the Year.* She whispered a foul word. Oh, how she would like to see him brought down a few pegs. He had the whole city thinking he was a paragon of social justice or something.

She used to think so too. She used to think he could do no wrong.

She didn't think so any longer.

"I'll make you sorry. So help me, I will."

She read the article a second time, her finger running down the lines, and as she neared the end, a slow smile curled the corners of her mouth.

Yes, he would be very sorry, indeed.

Two

"GIRLFRIEND, YOU LOOK FABULOUS!" SUSAN BALES, MY dearest friend in the world, gave me a hug and an air kiss. "That dress is to die for."

I loved Susan for many reasons, not the least of which was her ability to know the right thing to say at the right moment. I'd been nervous about my appearance tonight. I so wanted to make Brad proud. Now those worries were gone.

"Where's the man of the hour?"

"Oh, he's around." I let my gaze roam the lobby of the convention center until I found him. He was shaking a woman's hand and smiling as they talked. On his left were the mayor and his wife. On his right, the governor.

"I don't see him," Susan said.

"Over there." I pointed. "With the mayor and Governor Brown."

Susan whistled softly. "Wow. Will I get to meet the Honorable Mr. Brown?"

"Only if you promise to behave."

The governor was widowed, wealthy, and beyond handsome. My best friend was twice divorced, attractive, and looking for her next husband. I could see the wheels churning in her head.

She slapped playfully at my hand. "What fun would that be?"

"*Susan* . . ."

"Oh, don't worry. I promise not to embarrass you or Brad. I know how much this night means to you."

"Thanks." I swallowed a sigh of relief.

Just then, I caught sight of Emma and Jason entering the lobby, followed by Hayley and Steve.

"The girls are here," I said to Susan.

"You go start introducing them to the dignitaries. I'm going to mingle with the other common folk."

There was nothing common about Susan Bales. Everybody was drawn to her laughter, wit, and charm. It had been like that since we were in elementary school. Charisma with a capital *C*. It was a wonder she hadn't gone into politics.

Hmm. Maybe she *should* meet the governor. It might be a match made in heaven.

I gave Susan's arm a squeeze, then headed toward my daughters and sons-in-law.

"You all look wonderful," I said when I drew near.

It wasn't mere flattery. My daughters were both pretty although very different in looks. Hayley was tall and wispy, Emma, short and athletic. Hayley had an air of elegance. Emma was pure mischief with a dash of rebellion thrown in.

"You're right about the dress," I told Hayley after kissing her cheek. "No one would guess you're four months pregnant."

Emma, on the other hand, had chosen a dress that made her look farther along than her six months. I was certain she wanted it that way.

"What do you think of the tux?" Jason asked, pulling my attention toward him.

"You look dashing, dear boy."

"Hear that?" Jason placed an arm around Emma's shoulders. "Your mom thinks I'm dashing *and* a dear boy."

She elbowed him in the ribs. "Don't let it go to your head, buster."

"Mom," Hayley said. "Where's the ladies' room?"

I pointed in the direction of the restrooms. "Are you all right? You look a little pale."

"I'm fine. Just pregnant and feeling it." She turned toward her husband. "I'll be right back. Wait for me?"

"I'll be here," Steven answered.

Emma tapped my shoulder. "Mom. I think Dad wants you."

I turned around, looking for Brad. When our gazes met, he made a slight motion with his head, one that said, *Come join me.* I nodded, saying to Emma, "I'd better go. Will you—"

"Don't worry about us. This is Dad's night to shine. And yours too. We'll just bask in the reflected glory."

Awash in good feelings, I gave her a quick peck on the cheek. "There's a table reserved for you four up toward the front. Your father and I will be at the head table."

I left Emma, Jason, and Steve and made my way through the crowd, pausing when others spoke to me, thanking them for coming, shaking their hands.

"We think this is so wonderful, Katherine."

"Tell Brad how glad I am for him. I think he deserves this recognition."

"Perhaps your husband will come speak at our club meeting in the next month or two. Our group likes to support local charities."

As I drew close to Brad, he reached for me with one hand. I took it, feeling the warmth and the strength of his grasp.

"Here you are," he said, smiling. Then he looked at the man and woman standing with him. "I'd like you to meet my wife, Katherine. Katherine, this is Henrietta Martinez." He touched the woman's shoulder. "Ms. Martinez is the CEO of the Ponderosa Group."

"Hello." I shook her hand.

"A pleasure to meet you, Mrs. Clarkson."

"And this," Brad continued, moving his hand to the man's shoulder, "is Paul Kay. He heads up the Boise Valley Council of Christian Churches."

"How do you do, Mr. Kay?"

"Very well, thanks." He glanced at Brad, then back at me. "I was telling your husband that Mike Sorenson has nothing but good things to say about In Step's efforts to provide home owner-ship for the poor and disadvantaged. I agree with him that it's a great opportunity for Christians to be the hands and feet of Jesus. I hope more people from our congregations will volunteer to work with In Step."

"That would be wonderful. No matter how many volun-teers we have, we can always use more."

The doors to the banquet hall opened, and the crowd surged in that direction. Before I could become one of them, Brad drew me off to the side of the lobby.

"Let's wait a minute."

I smiled. "Nerves?"

"Some."

"Honey, don't you know? Everyone here admires you and what you're doing. There's nothing to be nervous about."

"You're prejudiced."

"You bet I am, and I have plenty of reasons to be." I kissed him on the cheek, making certain afterward that I hadn't left lipstick behind. That wouldn't do.

"Mom. Dad. Are you ready to go in?"

At Emma's voice, I turned to watch our daughters and their husbands approach. "We're ready."

"Good," said our youngest, "because I'm starving."

"You're always starving," Jason said, laughter in his voice.

"I'm eating for two."

Hayley gave her sister a petulant glance. "At least you can eat without getting sick."

"Ah, Hay. I'm sorry." Emma looked contrite. "I bet you'll be over it any day now."

I slipped my arm through Brad's. "Let's go in."

We turned in unison, but before we could take our first step, the bright glare of lights from a news camera blinded me. I put up my hand to shield my eyes but lowered it at once, remembering the need to look poised and calm when approached by the press.

"Mr. Clarkson, Greta St. James, Channel 5 News. This is a big night for you, a very great honor to receive the Humanitarian of the Year Award." She held the microphone toward Brad.

"Yes, it is."

"Certainly all the recognition and the articles in the newspaper should bring in more donations to your foundation."

"Well, we hope so. More funds mean we can help more people."

Greta smiled. "Yes. I'm sure. But Channel 5 News has learned of an allegation that In Step has mismanaged charitable funds in recent years. Do you have anything to say in response?"

Brad drew back an inch or two. "No, I don't have a response. I don't know of any such allegation."

"The paper quotes you as saying that it's more blessed to give than receive. But isn't it true that you personally receive rather generously because of the foundation?"

"I'm not sure what you're asking."

"Isn't that why you need to increase donations? To cover generosity to yourself and other board and staff members."

"No, that's *not* true." Brad's eyes narrowed.

While Greta St. James might not know the warning signs, I did. My husband was waging a battle with his temper, and I wasn't sure he would win.

"In Step is a faith-based charity. Most of your supporters are good people of modest means who want to help those less fortunate. How would those donors feel if they thought they'd been duped?"

"No one has been duped." Brad's grip tightened on my arm. "Please excuse us. We—"

"Mrs. Clarkson . . ."

I felt pinned by the reporter's gaze as she turned her attention upon me.

"You've worked with In Step too. Were you aware that there were questionable practices in regard to the organization's finances?"

The microphone came at me.

Greta St. James wore a red blazer over a white blouse. Her hair was black and fell softly about her face and shoulders. She was young, perhaps in her late twenties, and her lipstick was the exact same shade of red as her blazer.

Strange, wasn't it, that I noticed such things right then?

"Get that mic away from her!" Emma stepped between us, hands splayed before the camera lens, facing down the reporter like a guard dog. "My mother has nothing to say." She turned toward me. "Mom, I think you and Dad should go in."

Some men appeared and shepherded the reporter and cameraman toward the exit. I heard one of them say, "This is a private function," and that pretty young woman with the red lipstick and red blazer insist they had a right to be there.

"Katherine?" Brad drew me around. "I don't know what that was about, but whatever it was, it isn't true. There's nothing wrong at In Step."

"Of course not."

"The foundation's accounts are all in order."

"Of course they are."

He looked over my shoulder. A frown pinched his brow. "What I can't figure out is who would make such an allegation to the press? Why would anyone want to stop the good work In Step's doing?"

I grasped for a straw of comfort. "Maybe they misunderstood. Maybe it's some other organization with a similar name."

It had to be a misunderstanding. That and nothing more.

Three

I AWAKENED AT 4:13 A.M. AND FOUND I WAS ALONE IN THE bed. "Brad?" I sat up and turned on the lamp. "Brad?"

No reply.

Closing my eyes, I tried to sleep a bit longer, but the events of the previous evening began running through my mind.

After the encounter with that dreadful reporter in the lobby, nothing more untoward had happened. Yet the life had gone out of the evening for both of us. We smiled when appropriate. We laughed on cue. When Brad received his award, he said all the right things and thanked all the right people while I applauded and smiled. We looked as if everything was fine.

It was a sham, a pretense. The evening was ruined for us both.

I tossed aside the bedcovers and got up, grabbing my bathrobe from the foot of the bed as I passed by. The house was chilly at this hour of the morning, and I was thankful for the thick carpet beneath my feet.

Downstairs, I saw no light coming from beneath the door of the den, which meant Brad wasn't working.

"Brad?"

"In here."

I followed his voice into the living room. He stood before the large window, the drapes pulled open. Moonlight fell upon him, silvering his hair.

"What are you doing?"

"Thinking about last night." He looked over his shoulder. "I keep trying to figure out who might have made those accusations about the finances at In Step."

"The media loves a scandal. If there were any facts behind what that reporter said, we'd have seen something on the news last night."

He turned to face me. "I hope you're right."

I crossed the room to stand before him. "Of course I am."

He stroked a hand over my hair. A hint of a smile played on his lips. "Thanks."

"For what?"

"Being here. With me."

"Where else would I be at this time of the morning? Sleeping?"

He leaned down and kissed me lightly on the lips. At the

moment, it seemed silly that either one of us had let Greta St. James spoil our evening. Now it was time to put her completely out of our thoughts.

When the kiss ended, I said, "Want me to make coffee or are we headed back to bed?"

"Coffee would be great. I don't think I could fall asleep again."

I gave him a quick peck on the cheek and headed down the hall, flicking on the lights as I entered the kitchen.

This was my favorite room in the house. It had been designed with entertaining in mind. Plenty of counter and storage space. Room for more than one person to move around without getting underfoot. A large pantry. A spice cupboard. Two ovens.

We'd had friends from church over two weeks ago. Three other couples, including our pastor and his wife. It was fiesta night. Mexican rice and refried beans. Fajitas with beef, chicken, and shrimp. Tacos. Sour cream and guacamole, green peppers and onions. Mexican fried ice cream for dessert.

It seemed I could still hear the laughter as we gathered around the counter, filling our plates, joking about Mike's super-sized fajitas, teasing Stan for adding ketchup to his tacos.

What would they think if those rumors about Brad and In Step became common knowledge?

I gave my head a shake. I needn't worry about our friends. They knew my husband. They wouldn't believe any of it, anymore than I did.

Soothed by that thought, I ground the coffee beans, filled

the reservoir of the coffeemaker, and started it brewing. Then I returned to the living room. "It'll be ready in a few minutes."

"I'll check to see if the paper's here yet."

Coffee. The newspaper. A quiet time with my Bible. Then off to church. An ordinary Sunday morning, like hundreds of other Sunday mornings that had gone before.

Brad

HE STOPPED MIDWAY DOWN THE DRIVEWAY TO THE PAPER box, raising his eyes toward the heavens. The night sky was inky black and spotted with stars.

Why would anyone want to cause harm to In Step?

The foundation paid him a comfortable salary, but it wasn't exorbitant by any stretch of the imagination. It would never make up for those early years in In Step's history when Brad had put much of the profits from his construction business into the charity's bank account to keep it in the black. He didn't want his salary to make up for it, either. That wasn't why he did what he did.

Tomorrow morning, he would give Stan Ludwig, his attorney, a call. He hoped Katherine was right. He hoped Greta St. James had her facts wrong and that Saturday night was the end of it. But something nagged at him, a feeling that there was another shoe left to drop.

Lord, if there's trouble coming, give me wisdom.

He waited, still staring upward, listening for God's voice to speak in his heart. In his eighteen years as a believer, he'd learned that the most important part of his prayers was the waiting and listening.

As if it were yesterday, he remembered the day he'd read the verse in Jude that would birth his ministry: "And keep in step with God's love, as you wait for our Lord Jesus Christ to show how kind he is by giving you eternal life."

Keep in step with Me, he'd heard God whisper. *Show My kindness to others.*

That's what he'd tried to do.

He remembered that first year when he was getting In Step off the ground. It had required lots of faith and an ability to function well on fewer hours of sleep. He'd put in long days with his construction firm while Katherine cared for the home and looked after their girls—Hayley in first grade and Emma, at four, still home. After the children were in bed each night, he and Katherine had gone into the den to work and plan, strategize and budget, hope and dream. Not every vision Brad had for In Step became reality. Not that first year and not in the years that followed. There'd always been a need for more money and more volunteers.

But all the same, In Step had grown and thrived. Thrived enough for it to become his full-time ministry.

He remembered the sweltering August day in 1998 when that had become reality. The Realtor had taken them—Brad and Katherine—to see available office space in the Henderson Building. He'd known at once it would be perfect for the foundation. Katherine hadn't been as sure. She'd worried a lot about finances after he'd sold his business to devote himself to In Step.

He'd tried to assign one of the rented offices for her use so she could continue running In Step with him, thinking that would ease her mind about all the changes, but on that point she'd been adamant. Her place was with the girls.

Now Brad wondered if she'd ever understood how much he'd missed her at his side. Not that he'd faulted her for putting her time and energy into their children, into helping them grow into the beautiful young women they'd become. Not at all. But still, he'd missed her by his side. He'd missed being able to run ideas by her in the middle of the day. He'd missed celebrating little successes with her, having her with him when he interviewed new recipient families, getting her opinion on possible home acquisitions.

There were times when Brad longed for the old days, when he wished it were just the two of them again, dreaming away in the den.

Right now—as he waited for that other shoe to drop—was one of those times.

Four

~

I'd been a believer since I was a child. Unlike many people, I couldn't point to the calendar and say that was the day or the hour when I accepted Christ as my Savior. It seemed to me that I'd always been a Christian, that following God had been a constant in my life from the beginning. Not a very exciting testimony, I suppose, but I was thankful it was mine. Better that than the troubles I'd seen others go through before they found God.

Entering church that morning, I saw countless friends and acquaintances. You couldn't be involved in the same church for more than two decades without becoming part of a large family. Of course, nearly everyone had seen the article about Brad in Saturday's paper, so there were plenty of pats on the back and words of congratulation as we made our way through the lobby.

We were almost to the entrance of the sanctuary when I heard Emma's voice. "Mom. Over here."

I turned and saw her standing with Jason in the line at the coffee bar. I waved to let her know I'd seen her.

"Let's wait for them," I said to Brad.

He nodded, and we stepped to one side so we wouldn't block the doorway.

We didn't often see Emma and Jason at the first service. They much preferred to sleep in and go to third service. Sometimes I worried how the two of them would make it through life with their laid-back attitudes. But at least they were in church. During Emma's rebellious teen years, I'd sometimes despaired that she would ever live right before God.

When they caught up with us, Emma gave me a hug and whispered in my ear, "Are you okay?"

"I'm fine." I kissed her cheek. "How about you?"

She grinned. "Ready to go another round with that reporter if you need me to."

"I'm sure that won't be necessary."

"I hope you're right. She was awful."

A few more adjectives to describe Ms. St. James popped into my head, none of them charitable. Oh, how I would love to give her a piece of my mind for ruining last night for all of us. But I didn't want to dwell on such thoughts, so I took Brad's arm and said, "Let's go in, shall we?"

We walked to our usual seats in the center of the sanctuary, about ten rows back from the stage. From here we enjoyed a comfortable view of the pastor when he preached, as well as the screens where worship lyrics, pertinent Scriptures, and PowerPoint presentations were displayed.

Brad didn't sit right away. He shook hands, patted shoulders, and passed around a few hugs, smiling all the while. I swear, the man knew everyone, even in a church the size of ours. Unlike me, he never forgot anyone's name, even if he hadn't seen them in months. And he always remembered to ask about other members of a person's family.

No wonder everyone liked him.

As for me, I'd fallen under Brad's spell the first time we met. When he turned those gorgeous hazel eyes in my direction, God's warning not to be unequally yoked with an unbeliever went straight out of my head. My heart was done in by his charm and that thousand-watt smile of his.

Despite my disobedience, God showed great mercy. He'd seen us through those somewhat rocky early years of marriage. He'd given us two healthy baby girls, and finally he'd drawn Brad into the kingdom.

I watched my husband as he shook an elderly man's hand and leaned closer to hear what the gentleman had to say. From

Brad's expression, you'd have thought nothing in the world was of more interest than what the old man told him.

It was a miracle, really, the caring man Brad had become. His home life hadn't been the best when he was growing up. His father, Roger Clarkson, was successful in business but emotionally distant from his wife and three sons. His mother, Teresa, put up with Roger's philandering ways in exchange for the comfort his money provided.

Once, about a year before we married, I had reason to wonder if Brad was as caring and thoughtful as I'd made him out to be. We'd had a fight. A bad one. I no longer remembered what it was about. Something silly, no doubt. But for two weeks afterward he didn't call me. Then I learned from a friend that he'd been seen at the movies with another girl. Oh, how my heart twisted at the news. I thought I'd lost him. When he came to see me a few days later and asked my forgiveness, I was quick to give it; I couldn't imagine my life without him.

And in the end, my fears were put to rest. I hadn't been mistaken about Brad's character. Even before he came to Christ, he had a generous, giving spirit. He'd been a faithful husband, a loving father, and a good provider for his family.

The worship team took their places on the stage, and Brad headed for our row. He sat beside me and reached for my hand. As he squeezed it, he gave me a smile. My heart fluttered in response. I had much to be thankful for.

Five

ON MONDAY MORNING I MET EMMA AND HAYLEY AT THE mall when the shops opened at ten. Our first stop was the maternity store.

"Isn't this cute?" Emma asked as she held a pair of bibbed shorts against her belly. "Perfect for when it gets hot this summer."

Hayley rolled her eyes. "You'll not only look like you *belong* in a barn, you'll look as *big* as one." She poked through a rack of separates. "You're lucky. Since you don't work, you can wear whatever you want. I need clothes that are suitable for the office. After this week, I won't have anymore time off until I go on maternity leave, and I don't want to wear the same three outfits for the next four or five months." She glanced at the shorts again. "And I wouldn't be caught dead in those."

Emma gave her sister one of *those* looks, as we liked to call them—narrowed eyes, wrinkled nose, and a slight shake of the head. "Say what you want. I'm going to try them on." She disappeared into a dressing room with the bibbed shorts, a pair of slacks, and three summer tops.

Hayley couldn't find anything she liked. "What will I do when I get much bigger than I am now? I hate this part of being pregnant. I can't find any clothes that I like."

"You'll find something," I said. "This is only one store."

"Yeah, but I can't spend all day looking. The carpenters are due to arrive around two o'clock this afternoon." She drew in a breath. "I don't know why *I* had to be the one to use my week's vacation to oversee this remodeling. I tried to make Steven understand that he would be better at it than me, but he wouldn't budge."

"Would you like your dad to come over and check on things? I'm sure he would if you asked him to."

"No. That's okay. I'm just stressing. You know how I get."

Yes, I knew.

She pointed to a bench at the back of the store. "Let's wait for Emma over there." As soon as we sat, she said, "Have you heard anything more from that reporter?"

"No. Your dad thinks if she had anything substantial, something more than just a rumor, the station would have aired that piece from Saturday night by now. But he's going to check with

Stan Ludwig today, to see if there's anything he should be doing."
Just in case.

"Anything like what?"

I shrugged. "I really don't know. Looking into salaries. Making sure all travel has been well-documented. That sort of thing."

Over the past decade, In Step had grown beyond anything I'd imagined it would. The office had expanded until it took over one full floor. Every year more employees had been hired, and the volunteer base had grown as well. Computer systems and programs had been upgraded, and giving could be done by phone, mail, or Internet. Everything was much more sophisticated than it had been when I helped Brad with the office work.

The one thing I did know for certain was that Brad's salary wasn't out of line for the president of a charitable foundation. When compared with people in similar positions, his earnings were on the low side. So whatever Ms. St. James meant to imply wasn't true.

"Well, if it were up to me, I'd see if I couldn't get that woman fired."

I patted Hayley's knee. "Thanks, honey. But I'm sure that won't be necessary. Your father says In Step needs positive media attention in order to help the recipient families. We don't want to make enemies."

"It looked to me as if Ms. St. James is already an enemy."

Emma stepped out of the dressing room, clad in the bibbed shorts over a sleeveless top. I was thankful for the interruption. I was sick of thinking about Greta St. James. I would just as soon never think about her or see her again.

Part Two
REAL LIFE

Six

ON OCTOBER 28, 1983, AT 8:06 A.M.—FIVE MONTHS AFTER Brad and I were married—a 7.3 earthquake rocked central and southern Idaho. Twenty-five years later, I still remembered every detail.

On that morning, I'd stood at the sink, washing the breakfast dishes, the faint scent of bacon and fried eggs lingering in the room. Sunlight filtered through the yellow cotton curtains that covered the kitchen window. On the stereo in the living room, David Meece, one of my favorite recording artists, sang "Rattle Me, Shake Me."

How appropriate.

Although the epicenter of the quake was about a hundred

and twenty miles away as the crow flies, it felt as if it were right next door. Everything in the house jerked to the left—me included—and water splashed onto my blouse as I grabbed the edge of the counter. I was swaying back to the right before I realized it was an earthquake, too stunned to run for cover or move into a doorway. The rolling of the earth beneath my feet seemed to last an eternity. It left me feeling scared and helpless for days afterward.

What happened on that Wednesday following the banquet was like that earthquake.

I'd been to the gym, the bank, and the grocery store, and had just brought the last of the canvas shopping bags into the house when the phone rang.

"Hello."

"Mom," Hayley said. "Turn on Channel 5. Quick."

I grabbed the remote for the small television set that sat on the kitchen counter. A punch of the button, and the television screen came to life. I caught a glimpse of myself, looking like the proverbial deer in the headlights.

"Get that mic away from her!" Emma's hand flew up to obstruct the view of the camera. "My mother has nothing to say." Her hand came down seconds before she turned around, her body shielding me from the reporter and her cameraman.

Greta St. James appeared on-screen, but she was no longer at the convention center, no longer dressed in that red blazer.

Instead she wore a lime green cardigan over a white blouse and stood outside the glass-walled entrance of the In Step offices.

"Last week, Channel 5 News learned of a rumor regarding mismanagement of charitable assets at the In Step Foundation. As you saw in the clip, we approached Brad Clarkson and his wife on the night he received his award. Mr. Clarkson stated he hadn't heard the allegation himself. We chose not to air the footage you just saw since it was uncorroborated. However, we've now learned that a complaint has been made to the attorney general's office, and they are reviewing it to determine whether there is cause for a formal investigation." She glanced toward the lettering on the door to the office, then back at the camera. "This morning, I again attempted to talk to Mr. Clarkson. He refused my request. But I was able to speak with a former In Step employee."

The image on the television screen changed to a second film clip, Ms. St. James seated in what looked to be someone's living room. I frowned. The room seemed familiar.

"Tell us why you decided to come forward, Miss Schubert."

My breath caught in my throat as the camera turned to the woman seated on a sofa. *Nicole?* The remote fell from my right hand, clattering as it hit the floor.

Nicole Schubert. Pretty. Slender as a reed. Blonde. She'd served as the Chief Financial Officer at In Step for two years, and for a short while she'd attended the women's Bible study in our home. What on earth—

"Because I didn't want the public to be deluded. All is not well at In Step. Brad Clarkson may call himself a Christian and look like a great humanitarian, but he isn't who others think he is." She looked straight at the camera. "Brad and I became lovers while I was the CFO at In Step. He led me to believe he planned to end his marriage. But he lied to me just as he's lied to his wife and his supporters."

I sank to the floor, my back sliding down the cupboard door.

The image shifted back to Ms. St. James standing outside the In Step offices. "Channel 5 will air the entirety of my interview with Miss Schubert this evening on *Our View* at seven o'clock. Be sure to join us then." Her smile pierced my chest. "Reporting from the Henderson Building in downtown Boise, I'm Greta St. James, Channel 5 News."

The weatherman appeared on the screen.

"Mom, are you there?"

I'd forgotten the phone was in my left hand.

"Mom?"

"I'm here, Hayley." I picked up the remote and pressed the Mute button.

"Why would she say those things about Dad?"

"I don't know." My skin tingled. My hands shook.

"But the attorney general is investigating. If there wasn't some evidence—"

Call Waiting beeped in my ear. "I've got to go, honey. I . . . I'll talk to you later."

I hung up the phone. After a moment's silence, it began to ring. Caller ID told me it was Emma. I closed my eyes and waited for the ringing to stop. Finally it did.

I set the portable handset on the floor beside the remote, then covered my face with my hands.

"Why would she say those things about Dad?"

Brad would never have an affair. He loved me too much. He would never steal from his company. He loved In Step too much. He wasn't devious or dishonest. He loved the Lord too much. I would know if what Nicole said was true.

I jumped when the phone rang again. When I checked the caller ID, it showed Brad's cell phone number. I didn't answer. I couldn't. Not yet. I was still in shock about what I'd seen. I couldn't think straight.

I rose from the floor and focused my attention on the groceries, emptying the canvas bags, setting food to be refrigerated on the counter to my left and food for the pantry on the counter to my right.

Should I freeze the pork chops or prepare them for tonight's supper? I couldn't decide. The thought of food turned my stomach.

"Brad and I became lovers while I was the CFO at In Step. He led me to believe he planned to end his marriage . . ."

Knees weak, I returned to the chair and sat on it.

"Brad and I became lovers . . ."

No. I wouldn't believe it. I *couldn't* believe it. Not about Brad. About anyone else, but never about Brad.

Hayley

HAYLEY COULD SCARCELY BREATHE AFTER HANGING UP THE telephone. That a scandal like this would touch her family was unthinkable. Saturday night had been bad enough with that reporter slinging accusations and her sister behaving like a bodyguard, throwing herself between the camera and their parents. But for their dad to be accused of infidelity in such a public manner—it was beyond embarrassing.

At least she wouldn't have to face her associates at work right away. Here she'd been grousing about using a week of her vacation to supervise the remodeling, and now she was grateful for it. By next Monday, maybe the worst of this would blow over. Maybe the attorney general would announce there was insufficient evidence to support the complaint. Maybe that Nicole Schubert would admit she was a liar.

Wishful thinking.

Oh, to have the family name dragged through the mud like this. It was unthinkable, unbearable. Her friends would be talking. Her neighbors would be talking. Complete strangers would be talking.

Dad's so naive.

Hayley had met Nicole on a few occasions, and she hadn't liked her much. There was something about her that was off-putting. But her dad was so trusting. He gave everyone the benefit of the doubt until they proved they were untrustworthy. It worked for him most of the time. People seemed to rise to his level of expectation.

Not this time.

What was it the Bible said? *"Be as shrewd as snakes and as harmless as doves."* In Hayley's opinion, her dad wasn't very shrewd when it came to women. He leaned toward the harmless-dove, love-one-another side.

Could he have cheated on Mom?

It seemed an absurd question. But . . . on the other hand, there were all those stories about Grandpa Roger and his secretaries. It wasn't as if Hayley's dad hadn't had an example set for him. Her dad would be quick to point out that her grandfather hadn't been a Christian. To which she would answer, sometimes Christians were unfaithful to their spouses too.

If her husband ever crossed that line, she would be gone in a flash. Steve knew it too. Unlike her mother, Hayley didn't believe in fairytale marriages. She was too practical for that. Oh, she loved her husband, and she was happy with the life they shared. But if he ever cheated on her, she would be outta there. She wouldn't hesitate at all. Not even a second.

Seven

I DIDN'T ANSWER OR RETURN BRAD'S PHONE CALLS. NOT the first one, nor the third, nor the fifth.

"Kat," he said on his last message, "I can't leave the office until Stan gets here so we can go over things. Please call me when you get this message. I'll come home just as soon as I can get away. And if you caught that report on Channel 5, don't believe it. Trust me. I . . . I . . . ." A long pause, then, "Please call me."

But I didn't call him. I needed to be able to look into his eyes when we talked about Nicole's claims. When I finally felt ready, I drove to the office, arriving during the lunch hour. One look at the receptionist's face, and I knew everyone at In Step had either seen or heard about Ms. St. James's report.

"Is Brad in?"

The receptionist—her name escaped me—nodded. "Stan Ludwig's with him."

Stan had served as In Step's attorney since its inception. Brad and I respected and trusted him, and he and his wife were among our closest friends. It made me feel a little better, knowing he was here and involved.

"I'll go on back," I said to the girl at the front desk. "No need to announce me."

I walked toward Brad's office, head high, shoulders straight. I didn't want anyone to think I'd been shaken by Nicole's assertions. Fortunately for me and my acting skills, most of the employees were out to lunch.

I paused at Brad's office door, rapped twice, then opened it. The two men turned to see who it was.

Brad stood as I entered. "Kat. I didn't expect you to come down."

"I thought I should."

"You saw the news?"

I nodded.

He came toward me. "I would've come home if I could."

"It's all right."

"It isn't true, Kat. What Nicole said isn't true."

I nodded again.

He studied me for a long while, eyes grave, then motioned

toward our attorney. "Stan was about to explain what to expect next."

"Hi, Stan," I whispered, finally acknowledging him.

"Katherine. Sorry this is happening to you both."

I blinked back tears. I didn't want to start sobbing. Now was the time to be strong.

Brad took my arm and ushered me to the chair next to Stan.

Stan said, "I told Brad it would be best if neither of you spoke to the press until this matter with the AG is settled."

"Don't worry," Brad answered as he returned to his chair behind the desk. "We won't."

"Refer all inquiries to me."

I had no problem with his instructions. There was no way I wanted to face another reporter. Not for the rest of my life.

"So what happens next?" Brad asked. "With the attorney general."

"If the complaint doesn't include reliable evidence of a diversion of assets or gross mismanagement, the AG's review may end without further investigation. However, if they feel there *is* some reliable evidence, they'll conduct a full investigation, inspecting all documents and records in order to prove or disprove mismanagement."

"What would they look for?"

"Illegal use of charitable funds, diversion of donations from their intended purpose, excessive amounts paid for salaries, benefits, travel, and entertainment. That sort of thing."

Brad released a breath. "Then we should be all right. They won't find anything like that here. We've always had excellent bookkeepers—" He stopped, his face gone pale. "Nicole supervised the bookkeeper. Do you suppose she might have altered anything in our books before she resigned?"

"There's that possibility," Stan answered, "but it's unlikely. The foundation's books are audited every June by an independent firm. If anything was amiss, they would have found it."

I took a measure of comfort from his confident tone, even knowing that all attorneys must try to sound equally as confident with their clients.

"Why not ask your bookkeeper and CPA to go through the records for the last few years? Maybe back about five. They can look for anything unusual. That way you'll be ahead of the game if the AG proceeds with a formal investigation." Stan reached for his briefcase on the floor beside him and stood. "Don't let this worry you. It will be straightened out in due course." He gave my shoulder a light pat. "I mean it, Katherine. Don't worry."

I nodded without looking up.

Brad walked with Stan to the door. They exchanged a few more words, too soft for me to know what they said. Then Stan left. Brad closed the door behind him.

"It'll be okay, Katherine."

"Will it?"

"Stan's right. Our books are in good shape. If not, the auditors would have told us there was a problem. It might be an inconvenience if the AG conducts an investigation, but that's all."

I lifted my gaze to meet his. "Ms. St. James doesn't seem to think everything's in order."

"Ms. St. James is misinformed."

I didn't want to ask the question that burned in my chest, but how could I not? "What about Nicole? She said—"

"She's lying!" His words were loud and sharp.

I stared at him.

He raked the fingers of his right hand through his hair as he pivoted away from me, muttering something I couldn't make out. A curse? Surely not.

"I'm sorry, Kat." He moved to stand at the window, looking down at the street six stories below. "I don't know what more I can say. The truth is the truth."

When a man and woman have been together as long as we have, they experience ebbs and flows in their relationship, including in the bedroom. Brad and I were no different. There had been times, especially when the girls were babies and sleep came at a premium, when our love life was somewhat less than passionate or romantic. There had been other periods when we were as desirous of one another as newlyweds.

These last few months had been like the latter. Brad's expressions of love had made me feel as if I were twenty again, lithe and beautiful. He'd even memorized verses from the Song of Songs to whisper to me as we lay in bed.

"What a lovely filly you are, my beloved one . . . How beautiful you are, my beloved, how beautiful! Your eyes are soft like doves."

Unbidden, the thought came to me: *had he whispered similar words in Nicole's ear while she lay in his arms?* I shuddered, willing the traitorous thought away. I would not allow such poison to enter my mind.

Brad turned from the window. With his eyes, he begged me to believe him. I did. Mostly. No, completely. Of course, completely. He'd said Nicole was lying, and I trusted him.

I stood. "I'd better go home. I . . . I need to call Annabeth and cancel the Bible study for tonight."

"Do you think you should? You almost never cancel."

"I have to watch that news program. I need to know what she says, and I can't do that with the ladies there."

"Whatever she says, it'll be a lie. She was angry when she quit. She's trying to cause trouble."

Why would anyone do this, no matter how angry she is? It makes no sense. None of it.

"Kat." He walked toward me. "Are we okay?"

I don't know. Are we? Tell me, Brad. Tell me we're okay.

He drew me into his embrace, holding my head against his

chest with one hand, his other hand rubbing my back. I could hear his heartbeat. *Bah-bum . . . bah-bum . . . bah-bum . . .*

"Stan told us not to worry," he said softly.

"I know."

"So let's not worry."

"I'm trying."

He kissed the crown of my head. "We'll get through this. I promise."

We'd come through other storms of life together. Like the time we broke up about a month after Brad proposed. Like the several health scares we'd had when Hayley was little or those terrible times with Emma when she was in her teens. But we'd made it through, all of us. God had been faithful. I had to believe we would come through this too.

I did *try* not to worry after I returned home, but I failed. Abysmally. I felt brittle, ready to shatter at the slightest provocation. I sat in the family room, television on, ignoring the phone when it rang, dreading the approach of seven o'clock. Time seemed both to crawl and to rush by at the same time.

It was midafternoon when Susan arrived on my doorstep. "Why aren't you at work?" I asked—not the most gracious of greetings.

"I came to see a friend in need. I'll bet you're sitting around waiting for that show to start. Girlfriend, you need to get out of the house. Grab your purse. We're going out."

"Oh, Susan. I don't want—"

"I don't care what you want. You're doing what I say." She stepped inside, her eyes staring past me. "Is Brad here?"

"No. He's at the office."

"What about your Bible study? Is it still on for the night?"

I shook my head. "I cancelled it."

"Just as well." She flicked her fingertips in my direction. "Get a move on."

With a sigh, I went upstairs, where I brushed my hair, added a golden-hued eye shadow to my lids, freshened my mascara and lipstick, and finished with a spritz of cologne.

"Where are we going?" I asked when I returned to the entry.

"I feel like something to eat. Do you want to choose?"

"No. I don't care where we go. I'm not hungry."

I led the way outside, handing Susan the keys so she could lock the door behind us. Soon enough, we were in the car and on our way.

"How about the Cheesecake Factory?" Susan asked as we neared the mall. "We can have some sinfully wonderful dessert to spoil our dinners. I recommend lots of chocolate."

"Chocolate isn't the answer for every problem."

"Maybe not, but it's a good place to start."

I released another deep sigh.

"Maybe you should skip watching that news report tonight. It'll only upset you more."

"I can't skip it. I need to know what she has to say about Brad."

Susan pulled into the mall parking lot. She didn't say another word until she parked the car not far from the main mall entrance. "Listen. I'm probably not the best person to give advice on this particular topic. I haven't had much success when it comes to marriage. And besides, I'm never surprised when a man strays. I guess I'm more surprised when they don't. But if any man is capable of walking the straight and narrow, it's gotta be Brad Clarkson. Don't believe the worst until you know it's true—even if that's what you've seen me do."

My chest lightened. "You think he's innocent?"

"Look, I can't say anything for sure. I don't know Nicole. I only met her at that party you gave last fall. But some women don't care if a man's married, and she strikes me as that type. If she came on to Brad . . ." She shrugged. "Well, who knows? But I wouldn't jump to believe her first thing. She's obviously no paragon of virtue, and that's by her own admission."

Susan and I were different in many ways. I'd been married to the same man for nearly twenty-five years; she was twice divorced. I had two daughters with a couple of grandchildren on the way; she'd never conceived. I was a Christian; Susan trusted only in herself, with a dash of positive thinking and universal good thrown in. I liked to keep things serene; she enjoyed a good argument every now and again. I was a conservative, and she was a liberal. Most of the time, I was right and she was wrong. At least, that's what I liked to tell her.

More than anything, I wanted her to be right this time.

Eight

DON'T WORRY ABOUT ANYTHING; INSTEAD, PRAY ABOUT *everything. Tell God what you need, and thank him for all he has done . . . Fix your thoughts on what is true and honorable and right. Think about things that are pure and lovely and admirable. Think about things that are excellent and worthy of praise . . .*

That evening, I repeated those Bible verses to myself as I sat in the family room, waiting for *Our View* to air. The Scriptures should have made me feel better. They should have brought a measure of comfort. They didn't. Probably because I couldn't find anything pure or lovely or admirable upon which to fix my thoughts. Instead, I thought about Nicole.

Not long after she was hired at In Step, I'd learned Nicole loved live theater as much as I did. So I invited her to join Brad and me when we attended a production at the Knock 'Em Dead Theater. We enjoyed her company, and thereafter she joined us whenever we took in a show. Nicole was bright and witty. Her keen sense of humor never failed to make me laugh. And she was pretty too. I couldn't believe she was unattached at the age of thirty-five. There had to be something seriously wrong with the men who met her.

To tell the truth, I would have loved to fix her up with one of several bachelors I knew. But those young men were believers, and church was the logical and most natural place for me to introduce her to them. Since Nicole declined my invitations to join us on Sundays at Harvest Christian Fellowship and seemed to have no interest in Christianity, my desire to play matchmaker seemed doomed.

Then one day when I was at In Step, I invited Nicole to the women's Bible study I led. Much to my surprise, she accepted. I had renewed hope. She attended for four months. Then, right before Christmas, without any warning, she bowed out, saying she didn't have time to continue. A couple of months later—in February of this year—she quit her job with In Step. I'd tried to call her a few times after that but hadn't reached her. Nor had she responded to the messages I'd left on her voice mail.

Now I knew why.

Uneasiness churned in my belly.

Brad stepped into the room, drawing my attention. His face

looked haggard. He seemed to have aged several years since the weekend.

Without looking at me, he asked, "Did you set the DVR to record the program?"

"No."

"I might need to refer to it later." His gaze met mine. "For legal reasons."

I picked up the remote and held it toward him.

Brad settled onto the opposite end of the sofa. "Is your women's group meeting at someone else's home tonight?"

"I don't know. Maybe. I left it up to them." Wherever they were, they were probably watching Channel 5.

"Kat, we'll have to talk about . . . whatever we see tonight."

Looking at the muted television, I nodded. He was right, but I wished he weren't. I didn't want to talk about any of this. I wanted it to go away. I wanted to wake up from this nightmare and find things as they'd been, as they were supposed to be.

An image flashed in my mind. The annual In Step Foundation Christmas party, two Decembers ago. Brad standing near the Christmas tree, Nicole handing him wrapped packages to give to the employees. Her smile, a certain look in her eyes as she spoke to him. The way he smiled in return.

It's not true. I won't believe it's true.

On the television screen, the host of *Our View* appeared. A second later, the sound came on, and I heard him announcing the program's agenda for the night. The segment with Nicole Schubert would be last.

This promised to be the longest thirty minutes of my life.

Brad and I didn't move or speak throughout the program. With each tick of the clock, I grew more tense. The waiting might be the death of me.

And then it was on. There was Greta St. James, speaking to the camera, reviewing the history of In Step, talking about the humanitarian award, talking about Brad, talking about us.

"Respected members of the community . . . very public figure . . . the growth of In Step in recent years . . ." There was an odd droning in my ears. I tried to concentrate on what the reporter said, but the words seemed disjointed and difficult to understand.

Images on the screen continued to change. A shot of our house. A shot of our church. A shot of the Henderson Building. One of Brad with the mayor. Another of him with his construction crew outside one of the remodels. And finally, there was Nicole, looking composed as she sat on her living room sofa.

". . . Our affair lasted more than a year . . ."

I wasn't sure how long she'd been talking before those words reached through the haze in my head. A minute. Five minutes.

". . . I loved Brad, but I could no longer be a party to his hypocrisy . . ."

Like pages in a photograph album, more images flipped through my mind. Nicole, leaning close to Brad at the table when she'd been our guest for dinner. Nicole, always the last to leave after Bible study, waiting until Brad emerged from his den so she could say good night to us both. Nicole, looking flushed, sitting in Brad's office when I stopped by one afternoon.

The television fell silent. The screen went dark. The program was over. What had I missed?

Slowly, I turned to look at Brad. "She was in love with you. All that time I was trying to be her friend, she was in love with you."

"She *thought* she was in love with me."

Was that a confession of guilt? The words I never thought I'd ask were ripped from me: "Did you have an affair with her? Did you sleep with her?"

"No. Never. Nothing inappropriate happened between us. When I realized what Nicole . . . wanted, I suggested she find another place of employment. She left a few weeks later."

I hugged myself.

"You know me better than this, Kat. You know I'd never be unfaithful."

In my lifetime, I'd seen ministers and televangelists experience spectacular falls from grace after giving in to sexual temptation. Who could forget the scandals that wracked the evangelical community in recent decades? Some of those men cheated with women who worked for them. Some with prostitutes. Some—

I shuddered.

I remembered the wives. Women who expressed surprise when allegations were leveled against their husbands. Women who, at least for a time, stood by their men, exuding confidence in their vindication.

Wives who'd been wrong all along.

I'd thought them foolish or deluded. How could a wife *not* know that her husband was having an affair? How could a wife *not* know if his behavior was less than godly?

Was *I* foolish as well? Had I been deluded all this time?

No.

The phone rang, and I cringed. Whoever it was, I didn't want to talk to them. I didn't want to hear anyone ask, "Did you see the show?" Because behind that question would be another one: "Is it true?"

I fled the family room, hurrying up the stairs, through our bedroom, and into the master bathroom, locking the door behind me. My back to the wall, I slid to the floor and drew my knees to my chest.

God, why are You letting this happen?

The church would have to conduct an investigation into Brad's actions. He was in leadership at Harvest, and now there was a question of moral failure. What about the women who came to our home on Wednesday evenings? Would they think me unfit to lead them in Bible study? Would they be able to trust me?

Can I trust Brad?

I pressed the heels of my hands against my ears, wanting to silence the questions. I had no answers, wasn't sure I wanted answers, wasn't sure I wanted the truth. All I wanted was my old life back.

"Katherine." A soft rap followed. "Open the door."

"No."

Brad jiggled the knob. "Come on, honey. We need to talk about this."

"Not right now."

"Please."

"I can't. Not yet."

"Kat—"

"Go away, Brad. I need to be alone." I drew in a breath. "I'll be all right. I just need some time."

He was silent a long while, so silent I wondered if he'd walked away without my knowing it. But then he said, "I'll be in the den when you're ready." Another moment of silence. "That was Emma on the phone. She wanted to know if we need anything, if she should come over. I told her to wait until morning."

Okay, I mouthed. My throat was too tight for sound to push through.

I stayed there a long, long while. Hours, maybe. And the devil had a heyday, taking my imagination places I didn't want it to go. I pictured things I didn't want to see. I heard sounds and words I didn't want to hear. But neither could I take every thought captive, no matter how hard I tried. And I did try. Only I didn't know how to shut it off.

Finally, I went numb. My head. My heart. It was a relief to stop feeling, to stop thinking, to simply withdraw into a quiet corner deep in my soul and hide. I never wanted to come out. Not ever again.

Of course, eventually I had to rise. Eventually I had to force myself to my feet, my legs shaky beneath me. By rote, I brushed my teeth, washed my face, shed my clothes, put on my nightgown, and opened the bathroom door. The soft glow of a nightlight led my way toward the bed.

Brad was there, lying on his side, either asleep or pretending to be. I slipped between the sheets.

"Kat."

"Not tonight, Brad."

"We need to talk about this. You need to hear what I have to say."

Tears sprang to my eyes. A lump welled in my throat. "All I want to do right now is sleep. We'll discuss it tomorrow."

He rolled toward me, rising on his elbow. "Can you sleep with all those questions bouncing around in your head?"

"I mean to try." I turned my back to him. "Just let me have this one night. Please."

Brad

HE COULDN'T SLEEP, NOT WITH HIS THOUGHTS CHURNING, not with Katherine lying with her back to him, pretending to sleep. As he pretended.

Eventually, when her breathing slowed, exhaustion having overtaken her, he got out of bed and went downstairs. He turned on the television in the family room, the audio low, selected the recorded program on the DVR menu, and fast-forwarded to the last segment of the half-hour show.

There she sat—Nicole Schubert. To the casual observer, she must look cool and poised. But Brad wasn't a casual observer. He recognized the anger that simmered right below the surface. He noticed the slight tremor in her voice and the set of her jaw.

He'd known she hated him. She'd told him so that last day in his office, the day she resigned. But he hadn't known how much she hated him until now. How could he have guessed she would do something like this? Maybe if he'd expected it . . .

No, it wouldn't have made a difference. He couldn't have prevented it. He couldn't have averted the damage she'd do. Knowing wouldn't have stopped the doubts from forming in Katherine's mind when she heard Nicole's accusations.

All of those months he'd worked with Nicole. All of those meetings in his office. All of those evenings at the theater, laughing over the comedies, applauding the performances. All of those Wednesday evenings when she came to Katherine's study. He'd prayed for her eyes to be opened. Why hadn't he prayed for himself? Why hadn't he foreseen it would come to this? A wiser man might have seen it coming.

Father, I've made my share of mistakes, and I'm sorry for them. I should have been wiser. You know the truth, and You know what I should do about it. Show me the way.

He rewound the recording and hit Play again.

Nine

WHEN WE WERE CHILDREN, SUSAN AND I USED TO VISIT her grandparents on their farm near Kuna. We both loved it there. In the summer, we rode her grandpa's old saddle horse and went wading in the creek. In the fall, we loved to play safari in the drying cornstalks. One of us pretended to be a tiger, the other a hunter. The tiger would lie in wait, and when the hunter passed by, the tiger would spring from hiding with a roar.

How I longed to return to the innocence, the safety, of those childhood games. The fearful anticipation. The startled screams. The laughter.

The tiger lay in wait for me now, but it wasn't imaginary. I could feel its breath on the back of my neck. This tiger was real and so were my fears.

I was in bed alone when Emma arrived the next morning. Tenderly, she drew me from beneath the covers, helped me into my robe, and led me downstairs to the kitchen where, with a gentle pressure on my shoulder, she urged me to sit on one of the chairs at the table.

"Dad made coffee before he went to work. Want some?"

I shrugged, shook my head, nodded. I didn't know what I wanted. It was too much to try to decide.

A minute or two later, my daughter set a mug on the table and slid it toward me. "Here you go."

I looked at it, watching the steam rise in a swirl above the dark brew.

"This will all get straightened out, Mom."

"Will it?" I met her gaze. "How?"

She sat on the chair to my right. "You can't think the stuff she said is true. Dad isn't capable of cheating on you. Not with her or any other woman."

I saw them in my mind—the receptionists, the secretaries, the administrative assistants, the bookkeepers. All the women who had worked at In Step in the years since the foundation moved from our home and into the office building. So many women, most of them young and pretty, most of them idealists who hoped to change the world.

Most of them filled with admiration for Brad.

I remembered the easy camaraderie my husband enjoyed with everyone he knew. He made friends wherever he went. People loved Brad.

Women love Brad.

Emma grabbed hold of my hand. "Listen to me. Nicole is lying. Anyone who knows Dad the way we do won't give credence to what she says."

Ah, my dear daughter. Headstrong and opinionated, sometimes a rebel, but also an optimist who looked for the silver lining in every situation. Was she really so naive? Didn't she know that people would believe the worst, not the best? Even some people who knew Brad would believe the worst.

Do I believe it? My chest hurt. *No. Maybe. I don't know. I'm afraid. What if it's true? Why would she lie?*

Through the years, I'd sat with brokenhearted wives, holding them while they wept bitter tears. What had I said to them? What words of wisdom? Had I spewed platitudes or offered real comfort?

Platitudes. I hugged myself. *That's all I had to offer them. I didn't know any better.*

"Mom, I think you should get showered and dressed and come home with me."

I shook my head. "I have things to do." I always had things to do, although right then I couldn't think what they were.

"Nothing that can't wait. Come on. It'll take your mind off things. I've got some homemade soup and fresh-baked bread to warm up for lunch."

Run away and hide. That's what I wanted to do. I supposed Emma's home was as good a hiding place as any.

Emma and Jason's two-bedroom north-end bungalow was about seventy years old. It hadn't been in the best of shape when they bought it a year ago. But they'd worked wonders with a little money, lots of ingenuity, and plenty of elbow grease.

"How about helping me put together the baby's crib?" Emma asked as she opened the front door.

I shrugged in response.

"I'm worried, Mom. I've never seen you like this before."

Perhaps that was because her dad had never been accused of adultery before.

"You ought to *do* something. It'll keep you from going over the same stuff in your head again and again. Come on. Help me with the crib."

That was another platitude I'd uttered to friends in the midst of their suffering: keep busy and you won't think about whatever awful thing is happening to you. I no longer believed that. Nothing could stop the questions and worries and fears from circling in my mind, like vultures over a decaying carcass.

"Let's go to the nursery." My daughter's arm went around my shoulders. "I need your help."

I looked at her. "I've never been good with screwdrivers and hammers."

"Fine. You can read the instructions. I know you're good at that."

Anal-retentive was what she meant. That was what she sometimes called me. The dictionary defined the trait as "excessively orderly and fussy." I knew because I'd looked it up. But I was neither of those things. Yes, I liked to keep up appearances. I wanted my home to be neat, everything in its proper place, and I did my best to keep myself in shape too. But I wasn't excessive about it. Besides, was there anything wrong with wanting to do and be one's best for God? I preferred to think of myself as a woman striving to follow the example of Proverbs 31.

Who can find a virtuous and capable wife? She is worth more than precious rubies. Her husband can trust her, and she will greatly enrich his life.

Hot tears stung my eyes. My husband could trust me. But could I trust him? Could anyone trust him?

"Come on, Mom. I need you."

Emma drew me away from the window and into the nursery, where she commanded me to sit in the rocking chair. I obeyed without argument. What was the point? She wouldn't listen. She was determined to make me do this. She was determined to make me feel better.

"Here are the instructions. You read them aloud, and I'll put it together."

A large, now-empty box leaned against the closet doors. A crib-sized mattress leaned against the box. Other pieces of the bed were scattered around the hardwood floor. Emma knelt in the midst of it.

"Where do I start?" she asked.

Before Nicole's appearance on *Our View*, I would have loved nothing more than to help Emma with this. Before this nightmare began, I would have admired the stencils on the wall and commented on the color scheme of the room and *oohed* and *aahed* over the baby clothes in the dresser drawers. But now . . .

I lowered my gaze to the printed instructions in my hand. The letters swam on the page. I blinked, bringing the words into focus, and began to read.

By the time the crib was assembled and stood against the wall, a pretty yellow blanket draped over its lowered side, I did feel somewhat better. Emma had talked nonstop, covering a vast array of subjects, pausing only when she needed me to read the next item in the instructions. Her monologue worked, much to my surprise. I hadn't thought about Nicole Schubert or her claims about Brad for at least an hour. Maybe more.

"It's lovely," I said as Emma put the finishing touches—a teddy bear and a yellow pillow—into the crib. "You've done wonders with this room. With the whole house."

"Thanks." She stepped toward me and took hold of one of my hands. "Why don't we go sit in the living room? I'd like to pray for you and Dad. Then we'll have the lunch I promised you."

"Couldn't we just eat? I'm famished."

My desire to refuse prayer took me by surprise. Perhaps it was because I—the woman with the perfect life—had been the one who always offered to pray for others. I couldn't recall the last time I'd requested prayer for myself. At the close of Bible study each week, when the women went around the room, sharing prayer needs and writing them down, I asked on behalf of others: *"Please pray for my mother who is planning to sell her home in Arizona . . . Please pray for Harvest's pastors and their wives as they go on retreat . . . Please pray for our church's missionaries in the Philippines . . . Please pray for my friend Susan to come to know the Lord."*

If Emma guessed the real reason that I asked to eat first, she didn't let on. And she didn't give in either. "It won't take long for us to pray. Your stomach can wait."

As we neared the living room, I heard the soft chime on my cell phone that told me I'd missed a call. Emma must have heard it, too, for she turned to look at me and gave her head a slow shake.

"I need to look," I told her, "or it will keep beeping at us."

I reached into the pocket on the side of my purse and

withdrew my phone. With a punch of a button, I displayed the missed calls. Three of them from Brad.

"Come on, Mom." Emma took the phone from my hand and dropped it into my handbag. "That can wait. We need to pray."

I'd spent most of my life surrounded by people of faith, and I knew a few things about prayer. I'd participated in twenty-four hour prayer vigils, fasted, visited the sick and dying. I'd approached God's throne with the awe and respect that was due the Almighty, memorizing Paul's prayers from Ephesians for revelation and spiritual empowering, asking to be clothed in the full armor of God, seeking to be filled with the knowledge of His will. Sometimes I'd prayed the Psalms aloud, loving them for the poetic richness of language. No, I was not ignorant about the spiritual discipline of prayer.

But my youngest daughter's prayers were nothing like mine. Never had been. There wasn't anything formal or poetic in the words she used when talking to God. I imagined her crawling into Jesus' lap the way a small child does with her daddy, holding up the pinky that hurts, asking him to kiss it better.

That was how she prayed for me—with passion and abandon and complete confidence that her Father in heaven heard and would answer.

Ten

"Look. Dad's home early."

As Emma turned her car into the driveway, I saw Brad step out of his pale-green Tribeca and close the door. He stopped when he saw us.

The same emotional exhaustion that I felt was written on my husband's face. In any other circumstance, I would have hurried to his side, wanting to encourage and strengthen him. But this wasn't any other circumstance. This was what it was. Wishing wouldn't change it.

Emma turned the key in the ignition. The engine fell silent. From the corner of my eye, I saw my daughter glance at me but I didn't move, didn't acknowledge her. I sat still, scarcely breathing.

Emma got out of the car and walked toward her father. She stopped in front of him, said something, and then hugged him, holding him close, turning her head and pressing her cheek against his chest. He leaned down to hide his face in the curve of her neck and shoulder.

Brad and Emma had enjoyed a special bond from the time she was a toddler. I never minded. I loved seeing how close they were. I was thankful for it when Emma entered the teen years and began to push boundaries, sometimes annihilating them altogether. Back then it was Brad who could most often help her see reason, Brad who was able to stop her from running headlong into disaster.

Today their closeness bothered me. It bothered me because I was afraid she would believe anything he said. Believe him without question.

The way I've always believed him.

I reached for the handle and opened the door. Brad lifted his head, meeting my gaze as I stepped from the car.

"I tried to call you," he said. "I got worried when you didn't answer."

Emma turned to face me, one arm around her dad's back. "I took Mom over to my house. We put together the baby's crib and had lunch together."

"Sounds like you had a good time."

If I opened my mouth, I would begin to bawl. I could feel the tears behind my eyes, waiting to break loose.

Brad glanced toward the street. "Maybe we should go inside. The press were hanging around the office this morning. They might show up here next."

Those words turned the blood in my veins to ice water. I hurried toward the front door, reaching into the side pocket of my purse in search of my keys. Where were they?

"Here, Katherine. I've got mine. Let me." Brad placed a hand on my shoulder as he reached for the door with the other.

I pulled away from his touch.

He looked at me, and I saw my pain mirrored in his eyes. I was sorry for that, but it couldn't be helped. The door swung open before me. Brad took a step back, giving me plenty of room to enter without getting close to him.

I lowered my eyes. "Thanks."

Nothing had changed in the house in the hours I'd been away, and yet it felt strange to me—the home of another woman, another couple, another family. I'd spent years decorating it to my tastes, painting these walls and selecting each piece of furniture throughout the house, perusing catalogs, shopping for bargains. I'd chosen the new carpet when the old needed replacing. I'd worked hard to make this a home for my family and a reflection of Brad's success. But now it seemed foreign to me, a place filled with secrets.

Had I lost all the happiness I'd known here? All the joyful memories? Everything that made my life what it was, what it was supposed to be?

In the kitchen, I set my purse on the counter next to the small TV. A light blinked on the answering machine. One message, the tiny window told me. I pressed the Play button.

"Katherine, it's Betty Frasier. Listen, I'm so sorry for what you're going through. I know this must be hard on your entire family. I'll be praying for you. But I'm afraid I'll need to miss the Bible study for a while. Maybe I can return in the fall. We'll have to see. But I'll let you know. Take care and know I'm thinking of you. Bye, now."

So Betty was the first to leave. Would there be others?

I felt abandoned and alone.

I turned to find Brad standing in the kitchen doorway. Had he heard the message? Did he understand what was happening? But then, maybe I didn't understand either.

"Where's Emma?" I asked.

"She went home. She said she'll you call later."

I took a glass from the cupboard and filled it with ice and water from the refrigerator door.

"I talked to Mike this morning," Brad said.

"Sorenson?" Our pastor.

"Yes. I'm going to meet with him late this afternoon."

To confess? Oh, the traitorous thought.

I pressed the glass to my lips to take a drink, but my hand shook so hard I couldn't tip it upward. I set it on the counter instead.

"Will you go with me, Kat?"

"Maybe you should meet with him alone."

Brad sank onto one of the chairs at the table. "I need you there."

How was I supposed to respond to that? A part of me wanted to hear what he would say to our pastor. Another part wanted to remain ignorant. Because what if the truth was worse than what I imagined?

The truth would set us free, so the Bible said. I shouldn't be afraid of it.

I would have to go. It was my place to be at Brad's side in times of trouble. We'd pledged to be together for better or worse. I was his wife. If he asked me to go with him, I should go. I had to go, if only for appearances' sake.

"What time?" I asked softly.

"Four o'clock."

"What time do we leave?"

"About three thirty."

"I'll be ready."

That was a lie. I wouldn't be ready. Not for the meeting with Mike Sorenson. Not for what might appear in the paper next or on Channel 5 next. Not for what our neighbors thought. Not for what our friends thought.

Not even for what, God forgive me, I thought in the depths of my heart.

I would never be ready. Never.

Emma

EMMA CRIED ALL THE WAY HOME, HER HEART ACHING FOR her parents. With everything in her, she believed in her dad's innocence, but she also believed things were going to be hard for them. Maybe hardest for her mom because she was such a perfectionist. She cared so much about appearances and what other people thought. In Emma's opinion, her mom cared too much about those things.

When she arrived home, she went into the living room and sat cross-legged on the floor next to the ottoman, her back against the couch. With a tissue, she dried her cheeks and blew her nose.

She thought about calling her sister again, then decided against it. Hayley was too angry right now. She'd decided their dad was guilty and thought their mom should leave him now before things got uglier, and nothing Emma had said to Hayley could change her mind.

She didn't understand her sister's reaction. How could she doubt their dad, of all people?

But maybe Emma knew why. She suspected Hayley wasn't as happy in her marriage as she made out to be. She and Steve fought a lot. Emma had heard them on more than one occasion.

It was funny, in a poignant sort of way. Hayley had always been the golden child, the favored one, the daughter who could do no wrong. She'd been the best student with the top grades, had excelled in both music and dance lessons, and had married a rising young attorney from a family of established, wealthy attorneys. Hayley hadn't caused her parents one moment of worry.

Emma, on the other hand, had tried single-handedly to turn her parents' hair gray and had given them more than one sleepless night. She'd pulled when told to push, gone right when told to turn left. And when she fell in love, it was with a guy who spent his first years after high school as a missionary and now worked in an electronics plant.

Emma closed her eyes and whispered a prayer of thanks for her parents. Without them—especially her dad, who'd shown her unconditional love through the hardest of times—who knew what would have become of her? Then she thanked God for Jason. Many well-meaning friends and family members had warned them not to marry so young; on their wedding day, Emma had been nineteen and Jason twenty-three. But all of those people had been wrong. Every day their marriage grew stronger and their love multiplied.

Ironic, wasn't it, that the family's wild child should be the one with the healthiest marriage?

Ironic and sad.

Eleven

MIKE SORENSON HAD BEEN BROUGHT ON STAFF AT Harvest Christian Fellowship as the youth leader about thirteen years before. But when the senior pastor fell into poor health and decided to retire, Mike was unanimously approved to step into the vacated position. A large bear of a man with an outgoing, fun-loving nature, he had a room-rattling laugh and a preaching style that was fun and down to earth. His wife, Annabeth, was his complete opposite—petite, soft spoken, serious minded, and shy.

I'm not sure how I felt when Brad and I were ushered into Mike's office and I saw Annabeth seated in a chair beside her husband's desk. Waylaid? She wouldn't be there if they hadn't expected me. Brad must have called Mike.

I sat in the first chair I came to and kept my purse on my lap. It gave me something to hold on to.

Behind me, I heard Brad ask, "Did she call you?"

Mike answered, "Yes."

Who did they mean? Nicole? Surely she wouldn't call our pastor.

"I told her I had nothing to say to the media."

Not Nicole. Ms. St. James.

I glanced toward Annabeth. Perhaps I hoped her expression would tell me what to feel or, at the very least, how to handle whatever was about to happen. Her eyes were filled with compassion.

I heard the door close. Brad stepped to the chair beside me while Mike moved to the opposite side of his desk and sank onto the large black executive chair. His gaze moved from Brad to me.

"I'm sorry for the reason for this visit. How're you doing, Katherine?"

I held my head a little higher, sat a little straighter. "I'm all right." Did I look and sound as brittle as I felt?

"I know this week hasn't been easy on either of you, but I'm glad you came to see us. Perhaps we'll be able to discover what God would have you do. Let's go to Him in prayer, shall we?"

I bowed my head. *What to do? What to do about what? About Nicole? About Brad? About In Step?*

"Father, we come to You with heavy hearts. Brad and Katherine are hurting, Lord, and in need of Your holy touch . . ."

I don't know if Brad's hurting. Maybe it's a pretense. How will I ever know what's true and what isn't?

". . . Open our eyes and our hearts to whatever You would have for us. Give us discernment and wisdom . . ."

If I had any discernment, I would've known what Nicole felt about Brad. I would have sensed she wanted my husband. Stupid, stupid, stupid.

". . . Father, direct our words and our thoughts in the coming hour and in the coming days. We ask it in Jesus' name. Amen."

The prayer was over, and I'd heard little of it. But now that Mike was through praying, it would be our turn to talk. I wasn't ready. Not even close. My stomach churned. My hands were sweaty. I rubbed my palms against my Levis.

Mike leaned back in his chair. "Brad, why don't you start?"

"Sure." He glanced toward me, but I pretended not to notice. "I already told you what happened the night of the banquet with that reporter. Then there was the complaint filed with the attorney general, probably by Nicole, although I'm not sure we'll be told the source of the complaint." His voice lowered a notch. "And now there's her claim of an affair with me. I feel like I've been hit by a cannonball."

Me too.

"The thing is, I'm confident we can prove there are no

financial problems at In Step. It may take a while, but I don't believe any laws have been broken. We'll straighten things out with the AG. Stan knows how to handle the legal aspects. I trust him to see us through the mire."

He fell silent, and I knew he looked at me again.

"What worries me most is what was on the news last night and in the paper this morning, the claims of sexual impropriety. I don't know—"

My head snapped up. There was something in the newspaper? I hadn't thought to look at it before Emma whisked me off to her house.

"—how to clear my name. It's her—"

I interrupted Brad. "What did the paper say?"

He looked at me. "Pretty much what was on TV last night. They interviewed Nicole after the story first broke yesterday morning." He shifted in his chair. "I was told some magazines have sought interviews too."

Was Stan right to tell us not to speak to the media? It seemed unfair that only Nicole's story was being reported. Shouldn't someone challenge her, call her a liar, demand a retraction?

Unless, of course, her story was true.

Mike said, "Tell me about your involvement with Ms. Schubert."

I held my breath, hoping against hope that Brad could explain it all away.

"I hired her as In Step's CFO two years ago last January. She came with great qualifications and stellar recommendations. From the start, everybody in the office liked her. Katherine liked her too and invited her to join us when we went to a play or a concert. Nicole's young and attractive and sharp as a tack. Well, you know what I mean. You met her."

I couldn't believe my ears. Was he going to sit there and sing her praises in front of me?

"Mike, I promise you, I never treated Nicole any different than anyone else I work with, man or woman."

Brad knew how to be friends with everyone, from the governor of the state to the guy sweeping the streets. Whoever he was with, he was at ease, no matter a person's gender or age or nationality or creed. He treated each one with the same genuine warmth and respect.

Perhaps his charm and good looks had been his downfall.

"I should've seen it coming."

I don't know how much of Brad's confession I missed while my thoughts drifted, but those words yanked me to the present.

"I felt like such a fool." He raked the fingers of both hands through his hair. "Nicole said she loved me and wanted to be with me. She said I'd made her believe I felt the same way."

My fingernails bit into my flesh as I clutched my hands.

"I told her she was mistaken. I told her I loved my wife. That's when she . . . kissed me." He kept his eyes downturned, not looking at the pastor, not looking at me. "Katherine walked in a minute or two later."

I remembered that day I'd seen Nicole, looking flushed, as she left Brad's office. Was that the day she'd kissed him? Was that the day she'd told him she loved him? I tried to remember Brad's expression. Had he looked guilty or upset? I couldn't recall.

Brad looked at Mike. "A week or two later, Nicole came into my office again. She was angry, accusing me again of leading her on, of making me think I wanted her. God knows I've played it all over in my mind a thousand times to see if anything I said or did should have made her think that. But I can't see what. She said my actions would come back to haunt me. I guess she was right about that."

Mike grunted his agreement.

"She quit later that same day. I haven't seen her since. She tried calling me a couple of times after that, but I had my assistant take messages. I never returned her calls. I thought that was the best way to handle it."

"And you never told Katherine about any of this?"

"No."

"Why not?"

Yes, why not?

"I don't know. I guess I should have. But I figured Nicole would come to her senses. I thought with a little time, she'd forget about it." Brad turned toward me. "I'm sorry I didn't tell you, Kat. But I'm telling you now. I was never unfaithful. I swear it."

He'd kissed another woman and never told me. Even knowing I'd befriended Nicole, he hadn't told me. Did he have other secrets as well?

How separate our lives had become. Why hadn't I noticed it before this?

As difficult as it was to sit through the hour and a half spent with Mike and Annabeth, it was worse to go home. Worse to be alone with Brad. With him and the gaping silence between us.

After a supper of tuna salad sandwiches and leftover peach cobbler, I kept myself busy in the kitchen. First I cleared the table and rinsed the dirty dishes before placing them in the dishwasher. Then I took a dishcloth and the spray bottle of 409 and cleaned the countertops, the stovetop, the front and inside of the microwave, and the handles and doors of the refrigerator. Next I decided the floor needed a good mopping. Only when every surface sparkled did I stop my frenetic cleaning.

I glanced at the clock on the stove. It wasn't yet nine o'clock, much earlier than my usual bedtime. But I was exhausted. All I wanted was to get into bed and sleep.

And never wake up.

"Are you finished?" Brad asked from the kitchen entrance.

I turned to face him, stiff and cold. "Yes. I'm done."

"Can we talk now?"

"I'm tired. We'll talk tomorrow."

"That's what you said last night. You can't give me the silent treatment forever. We need to clear the air."

I sighed. "I don't know what you want me to say."

"It isn't about what I *want* you to say. It's about what you're thinking, what you're feeling. It's about what you *need* to say to me."

I didn't want to admit those feelings to myself, let alone to him. I didn't want to give voice to my doubts and suspicions, to my disappointments and fears. To say them aloud would make giants out of them, and I was clearly no David with enough faith to slay Goliath.

"Talk to me, Kat. Don't shut me out. We've never kept secrets."

My eyes widened. "'Never kept secrets'?" My voice grew strident. "What do you call kissing Nicole and not telling me?"

"She kissed me."

"That's putting a fine point on it."

"I'm sorry. I thought when she quit that the problem was solved."

"Looks like you thought wrong." I swept past him, wanting to get as far away from him as I could. *Don't follow me. Please don't follow.*

I got my wish. He didn't come into the bedroom then. Neither did he come an hour later or an hour after that or an hour after that. I know because I was awake, checking the clock every few minutes, until sleep finally claimed me somewhere around two in the morning.

When I awakened, the pink fingers of dawn were poking through the blinds and stretching across the ceiling. I rolled my head on the pillow to look the other way. Brad's side of the mattress was untouched. He'd never come to bed.

My gut knotted, and I began to weep. Silent tears at first, followed soon enough by sobs that wracked my body. I pulled Brad's pillow over my face, trying to muffle the sound of my heartache. Instead, when I breathed in, I filled my nostrils with my husband's familiar scent, and the pain escalated.

I loved Brad, but could I forgive him if he'd broken his marriage vows? Could I believe his professions of innocence? How would I ever know what was the truth and what was a lie?

So many questions.

So few answers.

Twelve

I WAS STILL IN MY BATHROBE WHEN HAYLEY CAME BY THE house, a little after eight o'clock that same morning.

"Is Dad here?" she asked as she followed me toward the kitchen.

"No."

"Did he go to the office?"

"Yes." I supposed it was true. He hadn't been there when I got out of bed, my crying jag spent. For all I knew he'd spent the night at the office.

"Have you had breakfast?"

"I'm not hungry."

"You should eat anyway. Isn't that what you tell me?"

I released a humorless laugh. "Probably."

"I'll scramble a couple of eggs. You go shower and get dressed. Then you and I are going out."

I'd sunk to an all-time low. I couldn't remember a time since the age of twelve or thirteen when anyone had to tell me to fix my appearance. I was the one who was put together in any circumstance. I was the one who took care of others, the one they looked to for advice, the one who maintained control even in chaotic situations. Now look at me.

I went upstairs and entered the bathroom, pausing in front of the vanity to stare at my reflection in the mirror. I looked even worse than I'd imagined. My hair was disheveled, my eyes red and puffy.

How did I get like this?

Nicole. Nicole had done this to me.

I saw my mouth harden, my eyes narrow, as anger overwhelmed me. Anger and hate. I hated Nicole Schubert. I hated her, and I hated Greta St. James. I hated Channel 5 News, the *Idaho Statesman*, and the attorney general. I hated what had happened to my well-ordered life, and I hated the fear and the tears and the uncertainty.

Before my eyes, I seemed to age, transformed by the malice in my heart. I touched the mirror with my fingertips. "What's happened to your life?" I whispered. My reflection didn't reply.

What man wouldn't choose Nicole over me?

That sick feeling in the pit of my stomach returned. Knees weak, I got into the shower, hoping the hot spray would wash away all thoughts of my nemesis. I wanted to be washed clean of her, once and for all.

In my heart, I knew I shouldn't give any validity to Nicole's claims of an affair, no matter whom she said it to. Brad's words should carry more weight with me. Twenty-five years of living with a man and serving with a man—twenty-five years of loving him and mothering his children—should count for more than accusations and innuendos.

Shouldn't they?

Yes, those things should count more. They *did* count more. And yet, doubt remained. It was like a small sliver under the skin, something I couldn't see but neither could I ignore, no matter how hard I tried.

"Mom," Hayley called through the closed bathroom door, "your eggs are ready."

"Coming." I wasn't hungry, but I would eat. Compliance was easier than arguing.

When I arrived in the kitchen a short while later, my hair still damp from the shower, I found the table set with my good dishes and place mats, cloth napkins in clear plastic rings centered just so on the plates. Scrambled eggs with diced peppers filled one platter. Another held crisp bacon and wheat toast. A pitcher of orange juice sat between the two platters. Soft music played on the stereo in the family room.

"You didn't need to go to all this trouble." I took my place at the table.

"I know, but I wanted to."

I would have done the same if the situation was reversed. My eldest daughter and I liked things to look nice. We found satisfaction in a well-set table, in the right mood and pleasant ambience. We enjoyed hosting parties, preparing food that was appealing to both sight and taste buds.

Hayley sat in the chair to my left. "Do you want to bless the food?"

"You do it. Please."

She obliged, taking my hand and saying a quick prayer of thanks.

I didn't feel thankful. I felt defeated, beaten, lost, confused.

As if helping a child, Hayley filled my plate with food and poured orange juice into my glass. I picked up my fork and moved chunks of scrambled egg around in a circle. My daughter let me sit in miserable silence while she spooned the remaining eggs onto her plate and spread raspberry jam on a slice of toast. I felt her annoyance. Hayley wasn't long on patience.

When her plate was empty, she patted her mouth with the napkin, laid it on the table, and slid her chair back from the table. As she stood, she said, "If you believe Dad was unfaithful, you don't have to stay with him. You can come stay with me and Steve until you get things sorted out."

Stay with her. Sort things out. Did she mean divorce?

"You can't sit around the house and mope forever."

"I'm not moping."

Hayley took her plate and glass from the table and put them in the dishwasher. Then she turned to look at me, crossing her arms over her chest. "Well, what are you going to do then? This stuff about Dad isn't going away any time soon. Those reporters will keep sniffing around."

"There wasn't more in the paper today, was there?"

"No, but there will be. You can count on it."

I put down my fork. I couldn't even pretend to eat now. "How can you be sure?"

"Because Dad's been in the news a lot over the last few years as In Step has become better known. They made a saint out of him for what he was doing in Boise and other places in Idaho. That's one reason he was named Humanitarian of the Year. Saint Brad. Do you think they don't love discovering he's a saint with feet of clay?"

"Do you believe it's true, what they're saying?"

She shrugged. "I don't know, Mom. His own dad didn't set him the best example in the fidelity department."

"Your grandfather wasn't a believer."

"True, but no man is as flawless as you've made Dad out to be, either. I love him. Don't get me wrong. I just don't think he's perfect."

"I've never said he was—"

"Don't bother to deny it. It's true. You're like a poster child for unrealistic marital bliss or something. You need to get your head out of the clouds. Dad's a man. He's human. And humans make mistakes. Even Dad. If he didn't make some sort of mistake, why is he in this mess now?"

Her words caught me like a hard right jab to the solar plexus. I'd taken secret comfort in Emma's unfaltering belief in her dad's innocence. To know Hayley had lower expectations made my own doubts worsen.

"I guess you're not going to eat that." She pointed at my plate.

"No. I don't have much of an appetite."

She looked at her wristwatch. "It's too early to go to the mall. Stores don't open until ten."

"I'd rather stay home anyway."

Hayley frowned, and her mouth pursed.

"I'm sorry, honey. I appreciate all you've tried to do"—only a slight exaggeration of the truth—"but I'm not in the mood for shopping."

"I guess I can't force you to go with me."

I shook my head.

"Then I'd better be off. I've got grocery shopping to do. We're having friends over for dinner tomorrow night, and I'm nowhere near ready. Why is it remodeling always takes longer than we think it will?" She moved to where I sat and gave me a quick peck on the cheek. "Call me."

"Okay."

I waited until I heard the front door open and close. Then I turned to stare out the window at the backyard.

"If you think Dad was unfaithful, you don't have to stay with him."

Brad was right. I couldn't continue to ignore him or the situation. The silent treatment would get us nowhere. Only I was terrified where talking might take us.

Thirteen

SECONDS PASSED LIKE MINUTES, MINUTES LIKE HOURS, AS I waited for Brad to come home. Numerous times during the day, I picked up the phone to call him. Every time, I set it back in its cradle without dialing. I wasn't sure what to say to him. I only knew he was right, that we had to talk. Talk until we were sick of talking, if that's what it took to resolve things between us.

But what if talking resolved nothing? Or worse, what if talking told me more than I wanted to know?

It was nearing four thirty when the doorbell rang. I don't know why I didn't check to see who was on the other side of the door. I usually did.

"Mrs. Clarkson." Greta St. James smiled at me as she placed

her hand flat against the center of the door. "May I have a moment of your time?"

I fell back from the doorway.

She moved forward. "We'd like your comments regarding the interview I did with Nicole Schubert. I trust you saw it Wednesday night."

My brain went blank. I wanted to turn and flee.

"Your husband has refused to talk with us, but we hoped that you—"

A camera pointed in my direction. I saw the little red light glowing and knew my reaction was being recorded.

"No comment," I whispered.

"Please, Mrs. Clarkson. The community wants some answers."

From somewhere within came the strength to move forward, forcing her to back up.

"Mrs. Clarkson—"

"No comment." I closed the door, twisting the dead bolt into place. Then I leaned against the wall and listened to the hammering of my heart.

Nicole must have been filled with hate to talk to Greta St. James. She'd tried to steal another woman's husband. *My* husband. Didn't she care how that made her look?

No. Of course she didn't care. Few enough did in this day and age. Actors routinely had affairs with their costars, and the next thing you knew, their relationship was being romanticized in *People* or some other weekly magazine. Token pity was sometimes shown toward the betrayed spouse, but never for long.

I felt the soft rumble of the garage door opening. Almost simultaneously I heard Ms. St. James shouting a question. Through the living room window, I saw Brad drive past the reporter and her cameraman. The garage door closed again, and silence gripped the house.

I waited for Brad to enter the kitchen through the connecting doorway. One minute. Five minutes. Ten minutes. Finally, I couldn't stand the tension building inside of me. I walked into the kitchen and opened the door, peering into the dim light of the garage.

"Brad?"

The door to his car opened. "I'm here." He got out. "How long have they been here?"

"Not long."

"Did you talk to her?"

"No. But I opened the door before I knew who it was."

He walked toward me, his footsteps slow, his shoulders slumped. As he drew near, light from the kitchen revealed the weariness written on his face. I stepped back to let him pass.

Where were you last night?

He stopped in front of me, as if he'd heard my silent question. His gaze met mine.

Many years ago, when I was still in high school, I heard

someone say that God fashioned Eve from Adam's rib because He wanted her to be strong enough to protect her husband's heart. Looking into Brad's eyes, I knew I'd done nothing to protect him since this awful mess began. Maybe I never had.

"So again I say, each man must love his wife as he loves himself, and the wife must respect her husband."

How often had I quoted those words to other wives? More times than I cared to admit. I used to think I'd followed that Bible verse, that I'd shown Brad the respect he deserved and needed. But now, in this crisis . . .

I lowered my gaze. After a moment, he released a whisper-soft sigh. A hot lump formed in my throat as I closed the door.

He walked across the kitchen to stand at the window overlooking the backyard. "Three corporate sponsors canceled their pledges to the foundation today. Individual pledges have dropped off too. Only a few days, and it's noticeable."

My heart hurt.

"I've been asked to remove myself from my position with In Step."

"Remove yourself?"

He turned to face me. "If I don't quit or at the very least take an unpaid leave, In Step might not recover from the bad press it's getting. There's already plenty of doubt in the public's mind. Especially in the Christian community. It's better for me to step down than force the board to remove me. It'll look better . . . later."

Another layer of fear swept over me. "Why an unpaid leave? You're the founder. You deserve better treatment. It's like you're guilty until proven innocent."

"How could I, in good conscience, draw a salary while employees face layoffs?"

"Layoffs? Is it as bad as that?"

He nodded. "It'll happen soon. I don't see how it can be avoided. Those corporate sponsorships were a big chunk of our annual income."

Perhaps I was selfish, but I couldn't help wondering how we would pay our bills if we lost his income. The mortgage, the car payment, the lights and heat, groceries. We weren't rich by any means. We didn't have unlimited resources—we'd put too much into building In Step through the years. We would be okay for two or three months. Would that be long enough?

Brad raked the fingers of one hand through his hair. "I'm the accused, Kat, not the foundation. If I'm out of the picture, giving might pick up again. Maybe some of those sponsors can be wooed back." His voice lowered. "The employees and the people In Step helps shouldn't have to pay for whatever I did or didn't do."

"But it's *your* ministry. You built it from scratch. No one knows it the way you do. No one cares about the people you help the way you do."

His smile was sad, his tone of voice poignant. "It's God's

ministry, Kat, not mine. I've had the privilege of serving in it, and I hope I'll serve there again. But that's up to the Lord. We'll have to trust Him."

His humility and trust shamed me. Could such a man cheat on his wife and lie to those who loved him?

I drew a shallow breath. "What will you do if . . . if you don't work at In Step?"

"I'm still good with a hammer." He held up his hands, palms toward me. "I imagine I can get a job in construction. Spring's here. New building has kicked into gear."

In Step had been birthed in Brad's heart. He'd never been happier than he'd been since selling his business and devoting himself full time to the foundation. Letting it go would be harder for him than he let on.

"I love you, Katherine."

Tears filled my eyes. His image blurred before me. *I love you too.* I wanted to say it aloud, but the words were strangled by the doubts I harbored.

He strode across the kitchen and took me into his arms, pressing my cheek against his chest, hiding his face in my hair. It was the first time he'd touched me in several days. The first time I'd let him get close enough to try. This time I didn't pull away. I wanted to be there, to wrap my arms around him and find security in his embrace. I hoped he wouldn't let go for a long, long while. Once we were apart, the thinking would begin again. The thinking and wondering, the dread and the doubts. Here, in the circle of his embrace, I didn't have to think.

Tomorrow and the day after that and the day after that, I would be forced to face reality. Tomorrow I would hurt because of the suspicions of betrayal. I would feel crushed by the words in the newspaper or on TV.

Tomorrow I might loathe Brad's very nearness, but for now, I took shelter in it.

Fourteen

THE NEXT MORNING, I AWAKENED BEFORE DAWN, MY HEART hammering, remnants of a nightmare wrapped around my throat, choking me. I gasped for air.

"Kat?" Brad's hand closed around my upper arm.

I turned my head. Even in the shadows of night, I knew he lay on his side, facing me.

"Bad dream?"

"Yes."

He drew closer, his head now next to mine on the pillow. "It's going to be okay." The fingers of his right hand twined through the fingers of my left. "It's going to be okay."

We hadn't eaten dinner the previous night. We hadn't watched the news or answered the telephone when it rang. Instead, we took refuge in our bedroom. We took refuge in each other. We took comfort in the old and familiar. And for a time, the troubles surrounding us retreated. For a time, I could almost believe my life was perfect once again.

But it couldn't last. Even my dreams knew that.

"I'd like you to go with me on Monday," Brad said, his voice husky.

"Go where?"

"To the office."

"Why?"

"The board meeting was called for nine a.m. I'll ask the directors to approve an unpaid indeterminate leave, they'll vote, I'll get my personal belongings, and we'll come home. It won't take long."

Although he sounded matter-of-fact, I wasn't fooled. His heart was broken.

He rolled onto his back and drew me closer, my head now resting on his shoulder. I closed my eyes and listened to the steady thrum of his heart. My memories were filled with thousands of mornings that had begun much like this one, my head near his, our hearts beating as one, words softly spoken before the start of another day.

Much like but not the same. Nothing would ever be quite the same again. Couldn't be. Nicole had changed all that.

I started to pull away.

Brad tightened his arm. "Don't, Kat. Please."

Had he held her the way he held me now? Had he stopped her from pulling away from his side, ever whispered her name in the dark?

Unwelcome images filled my mind. My nightmare revisited.

"There's no way I can prove what I say is true. There's no way to prove what she says is a lie." His voice was low, almost a whisper. "Unless she confesses the truth, it will always be her word against mine."

I preferred things to be black or white. That was my nature. I wasn't comfortable with shades of gray. But that's where I lived at the moment—in a world gone the color of slate.

He slid his arm from beneath my head, rolled to the side of the bed, and sat up. "I'm going to take my shower." A few moments later, the bathroom door closed behind him.

Outside, the sky blushed with the promise of dawn, staining the blinds a pale pink. Another morning I might have gone to the window to observe the sunrise. I might have hummed a praise song as I witnessed the advent of another day.

This was not another morning. I had no songs inside me.

I got out of bed and slipped into my robe. Bare feet carried me down the stairs. I stopped to turn up the heat to take the chill from the house, then thought better of it. If Brad was out of work for long, we might not be able to afford extra heat.

I leaned the top of my head against the wall next to the thermostat. "Jesus, I'm frightened. I need Your help."

Peace in the midst of a storm. Wasn't that what believers were promised? So why was I drowning in fear instead? Why did the future look so black?

I entered the kitchen and started the coffee brewing. Then I went into the family room to await the machine's final gasp. My gaze fell on the end table to my left. There was my Bible, untouched since the previous Sunday.

I lifted the leather-bound book from the table and placed it on my lap. I didn't open it, didn't turn on the lamp. Instead, I allowed the stillness of morning to surround me, and I hoped it would bring an equal calm to my heart.

Wisdom . . . Discernment . . . Patience . . . Strength . . . Never had I needed those attributes more than now. Never had I felt so far from having them.

Where are You, God?

No sound. No touch. No sense of peace.

Only turmoil. Only aloneness.

Brad entered the kitchen. I watched as he took two mugs from the cupboard and set them near the coffeemaker. He drummed his fingertips on the countertop, then turned and walked to the telephone.

"We've got messages on the machine," he said, punching the button.

The monotone voice of the recorder gave the date and time.

"Mom and Dad." Emma. "Are you guys home? Call me when you get this."

Click. *Bzzzzzz.*

Again, the monotone voice.

"Brad? Evan Daniels. I got the message about the board meeting on Monday. Think it's a good idea. We need to clear the air. But I'd like to talk to you before then if we can. Call me at home. I should be around most of the weekend." A pause. "Oh, and sorry you're having to go through this. We're praying for you."

Click. *Bzzzzzz.*

I hugged my stomach.

The machine again, reporting the time of the call.

"Brad. It's Stan Ludwig. Got your message. I'll be at your office Monday morning a half hour before the meeting. There are some details we should work through before you talk to the board. If you've got any questions or concerns, call me over the weekend. And remember to stay away from the press. They aren't going to let up. I suggest you stay close to the house until Monday. Might be a good idea to stay home from church tomorrow, just in case the media is waiting for you there."

Click. *Bzzzzzz.*

The coffeemaker gurgled and gasped. I forced myself to breathe.

Years ago, I heard a friend say to her husband, "Be careful what river you go down because I'm in the boat with you."

Today I understood what she meant. My life was joined with Brad's. When we married, two became one. What he did or didn't do had a direct impact on me. I was in the same boat with him. The rapids were rough, and water was rushing over the sides, attempting to swamp us.

Was there any hope we would survive?

Fifteen

WE DID AS WE WERE ADVISED, STAYING HOME THE ENTIRE weekend. We saw no one except for Emma and Jason, who dropped by on their way home after third service Sunday morning, and the pizza delivery guy who delivered our dinner Sunday night. We spoke little, both of us wondering what the next morning would bring, both of us sure it wouldn't be anything good.

On Monday, as Brad and I walked from the parking garage toward the In Step offices, I experienced true empathy for those women I'd seen on TV and in tabloids. Wives who entered courtrooms or made their way through a sea of microphones at the side of their embattled husbands. I realized they weren't always naive, foolish, or blindly loyal. Sometimes they were simply swept along by the storm of events.

Reporters and cameramen from newspapers and television stations—local and national—waited for Brad at the main entrance of the Henderson Building. I ducked my head forward, the way I'd seen countless others do in similar circumstances. I'd thought it was to avoid having their faces captured on film, but I'd been wrong. It was to avoid eye contact. If I didn't look at them, I could pretend they weren't there. I could ignore the questions they hurled at us.

"No comment," Brad repeated. "No comment."

His hand on my back kept me moving forward until we entered the relative safety of the elevator. I waited until the doors closed and the car moved upward before I turned around.

Brad gave me a repentant look. "I shouldn't have asked you to come with me."

"You didn't know they'd be here."

"It's why Stan told us to stay home over the weekend. So we could avoid them."

Okay, maybe he should have known, but we were in unfamiliar territory. Both of us.

The elevator doors opened. We exchanged another look—filled with trepidation—before we moved toward the glass doorway, Brad's hand once again on the small of my back.

All eyes were trained on us as we entered the In Step offices. A hush hovered over the large main room. This time I held my head high, my back ramrod straight, and tried my best to look calm and serene—two things I wasn't.

"Good morning, Sue," Brad said to the receptionist.

"Good morning," she answered.

"Morning, Kay."

"Good morning."

"Morning, Roberta."

He continued acknowledging each person as we made our way toward his private office. Once there, after he gave his assistant the same greeting, he asked, "Are any board members here?"

"Not yet."

"How about Stan?"

Lori motioned with her head. "He arrived a few minutes ago. He's in your office now." She reached out and touched his forearm. "I want you to know, I don't believe a word of it. Not a word."

He gave her a stoic smile. "I appreciate that, Lori. Thanks."

"If there's anything I can do . . ."

He nodded. "I know."

Lori Kendrick had been hired as Brad's administrative assistant about nine years ago. An attractive woman in her early fifties, she was totally dedicated to her job. And to Brad.

I could imagine what she wanted to do to Nicole Schubert.

Lori looked at me, sympathy in her eyes. "If I can help, Katherine, you need only ask."

"Thank you."

"I'd better see Stan now," Brad said, "but as soon as the board meeting ends, I'll need to meet with you, Lori. When the board members arrive, tell them we'll begin promptly at nine o'clock." He glanced at me. "Ready?"

I nodded, and Brad led the way into his office.

Stan stood when he saw us. "Katherine. Brad."

I sat on the small sofa near the door.

"Thanks for coming." Brad shook the attorney's hand before rounding his desk to sit in the executive chair. "Was the press here when you arrived?"

"Yes."

"Some mess."

"Some mess."

Brad glanced in my direction, although it was Stan whom he addressed. "What do you advise?"

"Short of suing Ms. Schubert for slander?"

"Yeah, short of that."

"Stay away from the reporters. And if you can't avoid them, keep saying, 'No comment.'"

I hated this. I hated every part of it. Was that really all we could do? Hide out or run away?

"What about the attorney general?" Brad asked. "What's happening there?"

"I believe they have everything they need for their initial review. Your bookkeeper and accountant have found nothing that raised any red flags, but they still have more records to comb through. Still, I believe you should be encouraged. I am."

Brad nodded, but his expression didn't change. He didn't look encouraged. "How long will the AG's review take?"

"I expect them to render a decision in a couple of weeks. Maybe three. If they decide a full investigation is needed"—he shrugged—"there's no telling how long it will drag out."

Brad glanced at me a second time, then back to Stan. "Will Nicole's assertions have any impact on whether or not they do an investigation?"

"Although it shouldn't matter, I can't say it won't, human nature being what it is."

Brad rubbed his forehead with his fingertips, his head bowed forward. Was he praying or simply weary of it all?

When he straightened, he met Stan's gaze. "This wouldn't be so hard to bear if it was just about me. But innocent people will be harmed. The recipient families. The employees. The contractors and subcontractors. The volunteers. If giving doesn't return to normal levels, staff will have to be let go. We won't be able to follow through with some of the home purchases. People who might have been homeowners by fall—" His voice broke, and he made no attempt to continue.

I hurt for him. I hurt for me.

"We'll do our best to minimize any negative effects for all parties." Stan opened his briefcase and placed a file folder on the desk, sliding it toward Brad. "I went over In Step's Articles of Incorporation and the foundation's bylaws, as well as your contract. As you expected, this meeting should be brief and to the point. And I believe we can assure your reinstatement once concerns are addressed."

It would be simple enough to address the public's and the board's concerns about misappropriation of foundation funds. Not so simple to address the matter of Nicole. Not if Brad was right, that it was his word against hers. As long as suspicion remained—

Brad checked his watch, then stood. "The board should be here by now. We'd better go in." He shook Stan's hand. "Thanks for standing by me."

"Glad to, my friend."

Brad moved toward me, and I stood too. He grasped my arms and stared into my eyes. Behind the strength, behind the courage, I saw the depth of his sorrow.

"This shouldn't take too long."

I nodded, wanting to say something to comfort him but at a loss for words.

He leaned in and kissed me. A fleeting brush of his lips upon mine. And then he left the room, followed by his attorney.

Tears welled in my eyes as I sank to the sofa a second time and reached into my purse for a tissue, determined not to give in to a fit of tears. I dried my eyes, sniffing all the while, then grabbed a second tissue and blew my nose. Finally, I sucked in a deep breath and released it.

Breathe in through the nose. Let it out through the mouth.

Breathe in. Let it out.

Breathe in. Let it out.

More in control of my emotions, I rose from the sofa and walked to the credenza to look at the many framed photographs that covered the surface. There was one of me and Brad on our last vacation to the Oregon coast. There were wedding photos of each of the girls and their husbands. There was one of Brad, holding a shovel, at In Step's very first home remodel project. Sixteen years ago. No gray in his hair back then. A few pounds lighter. Otherwise, he looked much the same.

Then there was a photograph of the entire staff taken at the annual summer picnic. They'd used it for the foundation's Christmas card last winter.

I picked up the photograph, my eyes focusing on Nicole. She stood behind Brad and to his right. I was beside him on the left. All of us were smiling. I set the photograph facedown on the credenza.

The sound of a man's raised voice caused me to turn. The office door stood ajar. I moved to stand in the doorway. Throughout the large open space that held the desks of many of the employees, people had stopped working and were looking in the direction of the boardroom. I followed suit.

Sheer curtains covered the glass wall of the meeting room. Through the light fabric I saw Brad standing at one end of the long table. Four men sat with their backs toward me. Three sat opposite them. Which one was speaking? I couldn't tell. His words were muffled, but not so much I couldn't detect his anger.

Judged guilty. By one man or by seven, my husband had been judged guilty.

And by me?

I hadn't yelled at him in public, but neither had I shown him unfailing support. Doubt and suspicion lurked in my mind day and night. He had felt it as surely as he heard his accuser now.

The boardroom fell silent. Perhaps one of the other men had intervened.

I looked away, letting my gaze travel around the central office. Many of the employees were young, in their twenties or early thirties. Most of them were women. A few talked softly to one another. Others appeared to be engrossed in their work, although I wondered if they were pretending. No one looked at me.

Did any of them believe Nicole told the truth? Or worse, did anyone in this place *know* that she told the truth?

I took a step backward, retreating into Brad's office, and closed the door.

Hayley

MAYBE HAYLEY WOULDN'T HAVE BEEN SO UPSET BY THE reporters if she'd expected them to besiege her in the same way they had her parents. As it was, she was taken by surprise by their presence inside the parking garage when she left work that Monday, one week after her father's resignation from In Step.

"What have you got to say about Nicole Schubert's allegations?" the reporter asked, his microphone at the ready. He didn't look much older than twenty-five or twenty-six. His cameraman was about the same.

She kept walking toward her car. "I have nothing to say."

"Is your parents' marriage a happy one?"

She studiously ignored the camera, her eyes fixed on the

ground as she quickened her pace. Her headache worsened. She'd felt lousy all day—achy, a bit nauseated, out of sorts—and she hadn't the energy to deal with this.

"Ms. Andrews, has your father had previous affairs with any of his coworkers?"

She wanted to ask how she was supposed to answer such a question. She wanted to call him an idiot and a few other choice words besides. For an instant, she wished she was more like her sister and could threaten to do him and his cameraman bodily harm if they didn't go away and leave her alone.

Nearing her car, she grabbed the keys from her purse. But when she reached for the car door, her hands shaking, the keys slipped from her grasp.

"Let me," the reporter said, bending down just as she did the same.

Their heads met in a teeth-jarring collision. Knocked backward, Hayley sat down with a grunt on the concrete floor of the garage. Stars flashed momentarily before her eyes.

"I'm sorry." The reporter, now wearing a remorseful expression, knelt beside her. "I didn't mean to do that, Ms. Andrews. Are you all right? Are you hurt?"

Her vision cleared even as her headache worsened.

"Here. Let me help you up." He took hold of her arm at the elbow.

She wanted to refuse but feared she couldn't stand without his help.

As the reporter pulled her to her feet, Hayley glanced toward his cameraman. No red light glowed on the camera. He'd stopped recording. Thank goodness for small favors. At least she wouldn't have to look for herself sprawled on the concrete on the evening news. Maybe the fellow with the camera didn't want the incident on tape for fear she would sue. And maybe she would, come to think of it. After all, she was married to a lawyer.

"Please. I am sorry." The reporter opened the car door for her.

She looked him straight in the eyes. "If you're really sorry, you'll leave me alone. You'll leave my family alone. We don't have anything to say to you." She got into the car and yanked the door closed.

This is your fault, Dad. Even Grandpa Roger never let his affairs get this out of hand.

Sixteen

SOME PEOPLE ARE LIKE THE PIRANHA, FIERCE PREDATORS with sharp teeth that tear the flesh from their prey. And many of those piranha-people spend hour upon hour online—on bulletin boards, on blogs, on social networking sites—dishing gossip, ripping strangers to shreds, feeding upon the wounded and dying.

Strange, how unaware I was of this before tragedy struck my family.

My introduction to the ugly underbelly of the Internet came through an acquaintance who, along with her e-mailed condolences, sent me a link to an online article that claimed to shine a light on the dangers and hypocrisies of religious charities. I recognized the bias against Christianity from the first paragraph.

The author of the piece brought up numerous scandals, some decades old, some more current. He used a lot of space covering financial misconduct, both proven and suspected, but I thought there was a particular note of glee when he discussed the sexual indiscretions of various ministers, evangelists, and church leaders—my husband included.

That now-familiar churning flared in my stomach. I should have stopped reading right then. I should have turned off the computer and walked away. But I didn't. I stayed, like an observer at an accident, craning my neck in order not to miss any gory details. Then, finishing the article, a bad taste in my mouth, I began reading the dozens upon dozens of comments that followed. There were a few calm and reasonable observations made. The vast majority of comments, however, were venomous, the writers desiring to get in a few of their own kicks.

The worst part was I recognized their anger as similar to my own. I'd entertained hate in my heart more than once in the past two weeks.

The sound of the back door closing caused me to start. I shut down the browser and left the den, not wanting Brad to find me in front of the computer. I didn't want him to know what awful things were being said about him by complete strangers.

Odd, wasn't it, that I doubted him one moment and wanted to protect him the next?

When I entered the kitchen, he was washing his hands in the sink. He wore a pair of Bermuda shorts and a white T-shirt, the back and underarms damp with sweat. His feet were bare, his grass-stained athletic shoes left on the patio.

Even after a week, I wasn't used to having him home in the middle of a workday. But it wasn't the day of the week that made his presence feel odd. It was the way we behaved around each other, the careful dance we performed whenever we were in the same room. A constant reaching out and turning away.

Brad shut off the water and dried his hands on a kitchen towel. As he turned from the sink, he noticed me in the doorway. Something flickered in his eyes. Uncertainty, I thought, although I couldn't be sure.

"I finished mowing the lawn."

"It needed it."

"I'm going to prune the shrubs now. Unless there's something else you need me to do."

"No. There's nothing." I glanced toward the refrigerator. "I thought I'd get a head start on dinner."

We'd been like this since the day of the board meeting. Stiff, formal, superficial. Talking to each other like a couple of strangers. For one night, ten days before, we'd found comfort in each other's arms. For a moment or so, I'd felt safe once again.

The moment hadn't lasted.

"Kat, is something bothering you?"

What a question! Everything was bothering me. "No. Why?"

"I'm not sure. You just look . . . different."

"Different from what?" I tried not to sound defensive. I didn't succeed.

"From when I went out to mow the lawn."

I shook my head. "Nothing's different." That was as close to telling the truth as I could come.

He observed me in silence, weighing my response. But finally he gave his head a nod, turned, and walked toward the garage. As soon as the door closed behind him, I went into the family room and sank onto the chair, clutched my hands over my knees, and leaned forward until my forehead rested on my hands.

"God, make it stop. This is too hard."

Oh, the wretched silence.

I'd never been bothered that God didn't speak to me the way He seemed to speak to others. The way He apparently spoke to Brad. A part of me thought believers were putting on airs when they claimed to have heard God's voice. I'd never made such a claim. I thought it presumptuous. I did my best to walk in obedience according to the Scriptures. I knew that pleased God because the Bible said so. That should be enough.

Shouldn't it?

I thought of the way Brad looked sometimes after a period of worship or following his prayer time. A look of joy that spoke of something beyond my reach.

Maybe my obedience wasn't enough. Maybe there was more.

The telephone rang, but I ignored it. I didn't want to speak to anyone, friend or foe, loved one or stranger. If I answered and heard the wrong voice, the wrong tone, on the other end of the line, I would shatter. I knew I would.

The ringing stopped. The caller hung up without leaving a message on the machine. That was a relief.

I sat upright and reached for a tissue to dry my eyes. I hated these tears. I hated the emotions that careened out of control. This wasn't me. This was someone pretending to be me.

"Katherine!"

The urgency in Brad's voice brought me to my feet.

"It's Hayley." He held up the cell phone in his hand. "She's bleeding. Steve's taken her to the hospital. Grab your purse while I put on my jeans and shoes."

I'm not sure how I made it from point A to point B, but sometime later I found myself in the passenger seat of the Tribeca, hurtling down the road toward St. Luke's Regional Medical Center.

"Father, keep her safe," Brad prayed. "Protect her, Lord. Protect the baby."

Please . . . Please . . . Please . . .

When we arrived at the hospital, Brad dropped me near the entrance to the ER and went to park the car. I dashed inside, looking right and left for someone who could tell me where my daughter was. Before I could ask, I saw Emma hurrying toward me.

"Is she here?" I asked. "Is she all right?"

"She's here, Mom. She's okay." Tears spilled down her cheeks. "But she lost the baby."

"Where is she?"

"We'll have to wait. They didn't want anyone back there besides Steve."

I feared my knees would buckle. It must have shown on my face, for Emma put an arm around my back and escorted me to the nearest chair. I sank onto it without encouragement.

I thought of Job at the beginning of his Old Testament story, one messenger after another arriving with worse news than the one before. *Job, your donkeys were stolen and your farmhands killed. Job, fire consumed your sheep and all the shepherds, too. Job, raiders stole your camels and killed your servants. Job, a wind swept in from the desert and collapsed the house, and all your sons and daughters are dead.*

Like Job, I felt like tearing my clothes in grief. I felt like falling to the ground and crying out that all God gave me had been taken away. But Job ended his lament with, "Praise the name of the Lord!"

Could I do the same? How did one praise God in the midst of so much loss? Once I would have thought I could do it. Today there was no praise in my heart. Only terror and despair.

Emma stepped away from me. "Dad."

I raised my eyes to watch his approach.

"Have you heard anything about Hayley?"

"She lost the baby." Emma took hold of both of his hands. "She'll be okay, but the doctor may want to admit her overnight."

Father and daughter embraced, Emma pressing her cheek against Brad's chest. He looked at me over the top of her head. I saw my own heartache mirrored in his eyes.

I envied Emma, believing there was safety in her father's arms. That security had been stripped away from me. I longed for its return.

Jason came through the ER doors, and Emma moved from her dad to her husband.

"I'm sorry, babe," he said as he brushed fresh tears from her cheeks.

"I wanted our babies to play together as they grew up."

"I know."

"I thought they would be great friends as well as cousins."

"She'll have other babies."

"But they won't be the same age."

Jason kissed her lips, then her forehead. "I know."

Brad sat next to me. I thought for a moment that he might take my hand. He didn't.

"Do you know what may have caused it?" he asked me. "The miscarriage."

I shook my head. "I haven't talked to anyone but Emma. Steve's still with Hayley."

Emma stepped back from Jason and turned toward us. "She told me she didn't feel well all day. Then when she got off work, I guess a reporter was waiting for her. Something happened, but she didn't tell me what. She was crying by that time, so I stopped asking questions." Emma fell silent as she lowered her eyes to a spot on the floor.

Could stress about her dad have caused the miscarriage? Brad's gaze told me he wondered the same thing.

I felt another part of what used to be "us" shrivel inside me.

Because of complications with the miscarriage, a D&C was performed, and Hayley was admitted overnight for observation. Only once she was in her room were we allowed to see her.

My heart felt like stone as I went to the bed and took one of my daughter's hands in both of mine. "I'm so sorry, sweetheart. I'm so very sorry."

Her face was pale, her eyes ringed in gray shadows.

"The doctor says you should make a speedy recovery. You'll be fine in no time at all."

She nodded. "That's what he told me too." Her gaze moved to her dad, standing beside me.

"How are you feeling?" he asked.

"Okay." Her voice sounded flat and lifeless.

"Is there anything we can do for you?"

"Keep it out of the news if you can." She turned her head on the pillow, closing an invisible door between herself and her father.

I didn't allow myself to look at Brad. I didn't want to see how he reacted.

A part of me felt sorry for him. He was a good father, a man who loved his daughters and was devoted to them. As busy as he'd been when they were growing up—especially while he was running his construction business plus getting In Step off the ground—he'd made time for his girls. He'd attended their school programs and made it to every parents' night, from kindergarten through high school. He'd helped them with their homework and encouraged them when they were down.

But another part of me questioned what I thought I knew about him. It questioned my memories and everything he'd ever done or said. Perhaps he wasn't the good husband and the good dad I'd credited him with being. Perhaps he was someone I didn't know at all.

Brad's hand touched my shoulder. "We should go."

I hated to leave, but I could tell Hayley wouldn't rest as long as we were there. "Yes. We'll go." I bent low to kiss Hayley's forehead. "I'll come again in the morning. You try to get some sleep."

"Okay," she whispered without opening her eyes.

Out in the hallway, I hugged Steve and told him to call if he needed anything.

"I will."

Brad gave him a pat on the back, expressing sympathy without words. Then he took me gently by the arm, and we walked down the hospital corridor. We were outside, halfway to the car, when I began to cry. Silent tears, streaking my face. No sobs. No whimpers.

And yet, somehow, Brad knew. He stopped, turned me toward him, and pulled me to his chest, his arms enfolding me.

Odd. It was what I needed and wanted, but still I tried to pull away.

He didn't let me go.

"Why?" I whispered. "Why did God take our grandchild?"

"I don't know."

"Why is He letting this happen to our family?"

He didn't answer. I sensed him pondering the question, testing his reply. But in the end, he only said, "I don't know."

Why, God? Why?

I wanted an answer, needed an answer. I wanted things to make sense again. I wanted to trust my husband. I wanted to have faith in the goodness of God, in the plans He had for me, for us, for our daughters and their husbands.

"Let's go home, Katherine."

Home. It used to be a place of joy. But now—

"It'll be all right. God hasn't forsaken us."

I wasn't so sure.

Seventeen

THERE HAVE BEEN OTHER SORROWFUL OCCASIONS IN MY life. My father died from a heart attack when I was in high school. A dear friend was killed in a car accident when we were in our early twenties. My favorite aunt and uncle went through an acrimonious divorce after forty years of marriage.

I'd been saddened by those events and shed tears over them, but I'd never let my emotions overwhelm me. Now everything overwhelmed me. The world had turned ugly, and I wanted to hide from it. Deciding what to eat for breakfast was too much to handle. Leaving the house seemed unthinkable. I moved around it in a kind of daze.

"You're depressed, Katherine," Susan said in her usual direct manner when she dropped by later in the week. "It's only natural, with all that's happened."

"I don't get depressed."

"Girlfriend, we don't get to decide what we feel. Feelings are feelings. They happen to everybody. And trust me. You're depressed."

I looked away from her, staring across our backyard at the bright-colored tulips that bloomed along the fence. Brad and I had planted those bulbs the first fall we were in this house. How many years ago was that now? Fourteen? Fifteen? I wasn't sure. Funny that I couldn't find the answer to such a simple question.

I wished Susan would leave. I was tired and wanted to lie down, to be alone. Besides, shouldn't she be at work? It was Thursday. No, Friday.

"You can't go on like this, you know."

"Like what?" I asked, looking at her again.

She motioned at me as if that were explanation enough. "Like *this*. You need to talk to somebody. A counselor or your pastor or somebody. It's no crime to need help working through a crisis."

I shrugged.

Susan leaned forward on the patio chair. "Kat, I'm your best friend. I care about what's happening to you. You've always been as solid as a rock for yourself and everyone else. We both know that. But you've been through a lot in the last few weeks. You need to let out all the pent-up fear and anger you've got going on inside."

I wanted to deny that I was afraid. I wanted to protest being called angry. But I couldn't seem to open my mouth. My throat had closed up, keeping me mute.

"I know you're worried about the investigation at In Step and heartbroken about Hayley's baby, but I don't think that's what's eating at you. You've lost faith in everything you used to trust. You've got to start believing in something or someone again."

I hoped she wouldn't start spouting psychobabble at me.

She laid her fingertips on my knee. "Do you believe Brad or do you believe Nicole?"

The breath caught in my chest.

"Do you believe God or do you believe Greta St. James?"

I stood and moved to the edge of the patio, my back to Susan, blood pounding in my temples.

She had a lot of nerve, saying that to me. I'd been sharing my faith with her since we were schoolgirls. Susan was the one without any faith. Not me. How dare she imply that I didn't believe God?

"Kat, I love you more than anybody. You know I do. We've been best friends forever. You tolerate me when I'm PMSing and when I just want to be ugly. You even put up with me during those awful days before and after my last divorce. Remember what I was like?"

Yes, I remembered.

"So hear me when I tell you this. I've been through it. I know what I'm talking about. You won't begin to feel better until you discover who you believe and what you want. Limbo is no place to make camp. You need to start working your way back to the real world, kiddo."

The world was real enough at the moment, thank you very much. More reality I didn't need.

Susan came to stand beside me. We exchanged a glance. I was the first to look away.

"You've had it pretty good, Kat. Great childhood with loving parents. You've always been happy in your marriage. You were able to be a stay-at-home mom, just like you wanted, and Brad supported you in that decision. If he ever objected, I sure never heard it. But what man would when he's being catered to by his wife?"

My gaze shot back to her as I opened my mouth to object, but she raised a hand to silence me.

"Sorry. That was the feminist coming out in me." She gave me a quick smile. "Anyway, like I was saying, you've had things just the way you wanted them. Until now, your kids haven't had anything worse happen to them than the sniffles or the flu. Your home is lovely, and you shine as a hostess. Seems like your God's blessed you for a long, long time."

"Yes," I answered softly.

"It's pretty easy to believe in Him when everything's going your way, isn't it? Not so easy when you hit a few bumps in the road."

I looked at her again. "It's not a mere bump when your husband is accused of a crime and may have been unfaithful and your daughter miscarries her baby."

"No." She shook her head, her expression sad. "And I'm not trying to be cruel or minimize how much you're hurting. But I am trying to make you think. Think or talk or scream or break something. Anything to get out all that garbage you're bottling up inside."

"I'm not the screaming type."

"No, you like to appear like you're all together. But girlfriend, you're not. Not all the time. No one is. Life happens to us. Things get broken, hearts included. We're kidding ourselves when we think we're in control."

"God's in control," I whispered.

She raised her brows and tilted her head slightly to one side, as if to say, *then act like it.*

Closing my eyes, I rubbed my temples with the tips of my fingers. I needed an ibuprofen. My head felt like it could split in two.

"I'm sorry if I upset you. I only want to help."

I knew that. I knew Susan loved me and would bend over backward to make things better if she could.

"I'm going to leave. I'm due back at the office."

I opened my eyes.

"Think about what I said."

I nodded.

She leaned over and kissed my cheek. "Call me." Her eyes narrowed slightly. "Any time, day or night. I'm here for you." Then she left.

A squirrel chattered from a tree in the neighbor's yard. A sprinkler stuttered on the other side of the fence. The day was warm, but it was pleasant in the shade of the covered patio. The air smelled of spring, unfolding leaves, thickening grass, budding flowers.

Spring. Life renewing itself. Fresh beginnings.

I raised my eyes toward heaven.

Help me.

I seemed to crumple in upon myself, and the next thing I knew, I was kneeling on the concrete slab, bent forward at the waist, my face hidden in my hands.

Brad

⸻

HE SAT IN HIS CAR, WHITE-KNUCKLED HANDS CLUTCHING the steering wheel. Beyond the guardrail of the overlook was a sharp drop into the reservoir. How long would it take to find somebody who accidentally drove into those deep, murky waters? The spring runoff had filled Lucky Peak to capacity. It could take days to find a missing car if it was going fast enough when it hit the railing.

The thought seemed momentarily inviting. He'd lost two of the things that mattered most to him—the love and trust of his wife, the respect of his friends and colleagues. He didn't know if he could ever win those things back. And if he couldn't?

He'd reached the end of himself and had nowhere left to turn.

He couldn't turn to Katherine. She'd made that clear enough. The same with Hayley. Among the members of his immediate family, only Emma remained steadfastly in his corner. Some men he'd considered good friends—his Christian brothers—had withdrawn from him as well. And it hurt.

Not that he would actually take his own life. He trusted God too much for that. But right now he understood why some gave in to the temptation. His life seemed broken beyond repair, his strength used up.

God help me. He looked up at the sky, piercing blue spotted with cotton ball clouds. "What do I do now?"

He hadn't found a job yet and time weighed heavy on his hands. He wasn't used to being idle. He'd lived at full throttle for too many years. Now when he got up in the morning, very little lay before him besides wondering how to put his life, his marriage, his family back together again.

No, suicide wasn't the answer, but he thought this would be a fine time for the Lord to return.

Come, Lord Jesus.

He looked one more time at the guardrail, then turned the key in the ignition, put the car in drive, and pulled out of the parking area.

Eighteen

A TOSSED GREEN SALAD WAITED IN THE REFRIGERATOR next to the deviled eggs and two steaks. I glanced at the clock on the stove, wondering if I should start the grill. That was Brad's job, but he wasn't home.

Where is he?

He'd left the house early this morning to fill out more job applications. Maybe he'd found work. What a relief that would be. I felt anxious every time I opened the checkbook, uncertain when we would see some income again.

Maybe I should look for work too.

Doing what? I had some office skills but nothing that would look impressive on a résumé. My proficiency on the computer had been acquired at home on my own time. Even my work for In Step had been as a volunteer. I hadn't drawn a salary since I quit a waitressing job soon after I became pregnant with Hayley—I was twenty-one at the time. Who would be interested in a forty-five-year-old housewife whose last place of employment was a local diner more than two decades ago? Burger King? McDonald's?

I shuddered.

Susan was right. I'd lived exactly the life I wanted. I'd chosen marriage instead of a college degree. I'd chosen babies instead of a career. Maybe I was a throwback to another era, but I'd loved my old-fashioned life as a wife, mom, and homemaker. I wouldn't have changed a single thing.

Now I wondered, had I made a mistake? Other women, like Susan, could support themselves. They'd worked their way up the corporate ladder. They weren't dependent upon husbands.

Like Nicole.

Oh, how I hated her. How I wished I could rid my mind of her, once and for all. I would have done it if I knew how. But thoughts of her hovered around the edges of my life, every minute, every second of every day.

Did Brad think about her, too?

"Stop it!" I slammed my right fist down on the kitchen counter. Pain shot up my arm. I groaned as I shook my hand, mad at myself, mad at my husband, mad at the world.

Mad at God.

My marriage was in crisis. Our livelihood had vanished. My husband may have lied to me, may have broken trust with the community. Hayley had lost her baby. My life made no sense to me, and I was used to things making sense.

Susan's voice taunted me again: "*It's pretty easy to believe in Him when everything's going your way, isn't it?*" Even hours later, the words hadn't lost their sting. Worse still, I feared she might be right. I feared my faith was weak, too weak to withstand the onslaught of trouble.

This time it was the words of the apostle James that taunted me: *whenever trouble comes your way, let it be an opportunity for joy.*

I used to think I knew what that looked like, but I didn't. I had no clue how to feel joy over or in my present circumstances. No clue at all.

The closing of the door drew me around. My gaze met Brad's as he stepped into the kitchen. I didn't need to ask if he'd found work. I could tell by the look on his face that he hadn't.

I asked anyway. "No luck?"

"No luck."

"I didn't think you'd be gone so long."

"I stopped by the church. I wanted to talk to Mike about . . . something, but he wasn't in. Then I got asked to work with some volunteers in the benevolence garden." He looked at the palms of his hands. "It felt good to do something physical."

Did Brad consider his current troubles an opportunity for joy?

I turned toward the kitchen counter. "I've got steaks ready to barbecue."

"Good. I'm famished. I didn't take time to eat lunch. I'll fire up the grill and then go wash up."

"Okay." I set several tomatoes in the sink and turned on the cold water to rinse them. By the time I looked over my shoulder again, Brad had disappeared.

I let out a deep breath.

I hated the way I was around him. When he was gone, I wanted him home. I wanted to know where he was and what he was doing every instant. But when he was with me, it wasn't any better. I remained anxious and tense. Part of me feared he would reach for me, want to hold me, want to kiss me. I'd let him do that when I shouldn't have. Because it felt like another lie. It felt as if I were promising things would get better between us, and I didn't know if it was true.

I reached for a knife and sliced the tomatoes on the granite countertop, wishing I knew what tomorrow would bring, wishing I knew how this would all end.

Nineteen

IT WAS MOTHER'S DAY, BUT I DIDN'T GO TO CHURCH. SINCE the last Sunday I was there—three weeks earlier—our private lives had become public knowledge, unflattering information splashed across television screens and newspaper columns. I wasn't ready to look members of the congregation in the eye. Not yet.

"I should be able to do what I want on Mother's Day," I'd told Emma over the phone on Saturday, "and what I want is to stay home."

"Jason and I were going to take you and Dad out for brunch after church."

"I'd rather stay home. I don't want to risk running into reporters."

"Hayley and Steve are coming, too."

"Your sister isn't up to going out. It's much too soon after her miscarriage."

"Didn't you know, Mom? She's going back to work on Monday."

"No. I didn't know. She didn't tell me when I talked to her. When did she make that decision? Has she—"

"Her doctor said it was all right. So you see, it won't hurt her to go out to eat with the family tomorrow. We could all go to second service and then to brunch afterward."

"Except I don't want to go. Not to church and not out to eat."

"But Mom—"

"No, Emma. Not this year."

She'd tried several more times to convince me, but in the end, I had my way. She'd been none too happy by the time she hung up the phone.

Brad hadn't been happy either. Only, unlike our youngest daughter, he hadn't wasted his breath trying to change my mind. I suppose he'd recognized the stubborn set of my chin.

Come Sunday morning, with Brad off to church solo, I wandered around the house, feeling restless and taking no pleasure in the solitude. Maybe I should have gone. Anyone at church who was prone to gossip would gossip anyway, maybe even more when they saw Brad without me.

After walking into the kitchen for the fifth time in half an hour, I poured myself a cup of coffee, then moved to the telephone, thinking I might call Susan. I picked up the cordless handset, set it down, picked it up again. It was early. She'd said I could call anytime, but I knew she liked to sleep in on the weekends. I should wait a while.

Telephone in one hand, coffee cup in the other, I walked to the easy chair in the family room and sank onto it. I blew across the surface of the hot beverage before taking several sips. My eyes went to the face of the phone. Fifty-seven calls in the log, the screen said. With my thumb, I began to scroll through the log in order to clear the screen. Susan's name and number. Emma's name and number. Hayley. Susan again. In Step. Emma again. Harvest Christian. Emma. Harvest Christian. Brad's cell phone. Stan Ludwig's office. In Step. Susan. Emma.

N Schubert.

I was several numbers past it before the name registered. I moved my thumb and scrolled backward.

N Schubert 10:23A May 6

Nicole called *here*? I glanced at the calendar. May 6. Tuesday morning, the day after Hayley miscarried. Were Brad and I at home when the call came or at the hospital? I couldn't remember.

I set aside the phone and coffee cup and massaged my temples.

I couldn't believe she had the nerve to call after what she'd said to the media. What gall! What on earth could she want? To apologize? Not likely. To talk to me? Never. To talk to Brad? Yes, that would be the reason for her call. She'd wanted to talk to Brad. She must have called our home dozens of times in the past two years, and I'd never suspected a thing.

A hard lump formed in my stomach. Had Brad taken this call and not told me?

I stood and hurried into the kitchen where I grabbed my purse and keys on my way out. I almost didn't give the garage door time to rise before I started the engine and slipped the gear into reverse. God alone knows if I looked behind me before backing into the street, or if I stopped at red lights, or if I looked both ways when going through intersections.

I drove aimlessly, no destination in mind. My eyes were dry, my heart cold.

She'd come into my home, even attended my Bible study. She'd pretended to be my friend. But it wasn't friendship she was after. It was my husband.

It appeared she was after him still.

Should I let her have him?

The pain in my heart was sharp, and I groaned aloud as I pulled onto a side street and parked at the curb.

Does he want her?

He said he didn't. Could I believe him?

I *should* believe him. There must be something wrong in our marriage that my trust could be so easily shaken.

But was Brad the cause?

Or was the problem with me?

It was early evening before I returned home. Brad opened the front door as I pulled into the drive. I stopped without entering the garage. When our gazes met, I turned the key, silencing the motor.

"Are you all right?" he asked as I stepped from the car.

I shook my head, nodded, shrugged.

"I tried to call you." He came toward me, stopping midway between me and the front stoop.

"My cell wasn't on."

"Where'd you go?"

"For a drive. I needed to think."

"That was a mighty long drive. You've been gone for hours." His voice lowered. "I was worried, Kat."

"I'm sorry."

"Have you eaten?"

I shook my head.

"I'll make you a sandwich."

"I'm not hungry."

A frown furrowed his brow.

There were more creases around his eyes and mouth than had been there a month ago. Maybe more gray hair at his temples, too. And his shoulders seemed bent under some unseen weight.

"She called here, Brad."

"Who?"

"Nicole."

His eyes widened. "You talked to her?"

"No." A pause, then, "Did you?"

"No. I thought you said . . ." He shook his head. "When did she call?"

"Last Tuesday. I saw her number on the caller ID."

He said something beneath his breath, then he turned and walked into the house. I closed the car door and followed after him. He stood waiting for me in the kitchen, his hands shoved in the back pockets of his jeans. Something about his stance made me nervous.

"We can't go on like this." His voice was low, somber.

I almost asked what he meant, but the words stuck in my throat. I couldn't ask. I knew what he meant.

"What's made you distrust me this much?"

"I don't—" I stopped. Saying I didn't distrust him would be a lie.

"You don't what?"

"I don't . . . know."

He turned and placed the flat of his hands on the counter, leaning into them, head bowed.

Did he pray? Probably. But I didn't. My heart was like stone, my prayers silenced.

I'd loved Brad more than half my life. He'd been my friend, my husband, my coworker, my lover. He knew some of my secrets, most of my sins, and all of my dreams.

Did I know him in the same way? A month ago I would have said yes. Today I didn't know what to answer.

"I can take everything else, Kat. I can take losing In Step. I can take the gossip and the garbage in the media. But I can't take what's happening between us. If you don't believe in me, I'm done for."

"I'm trying."

He turned to face me. "You shouldn't have to try. You should *know*."

"I'm doing the best I can."

Something in his eyes made me wonder if my best would be good enough.

Emma

On Wednesday, Emma met her dad for lunch at Applebee's.

"My treat," she told him as they slipped into the booth.

"I think I can still afford to buy my daughter lunch."

"I don't care. This is my treat."

He chuckled. "Okay. I can tell when it's useless to argue with you."

"Good." She opened the menu, then looked at him again. "How's the job hunt going?"

"Not great. I thought I'd have something by now. I don't feel old, but that's how a lot of employers look at me. Maybe they're unsure if I can handle the physical labor after so many years behind a desk."

"You're *not* old. One look at you and they can see that."

He patted the back of one of her hands against the table. "Thanks, honey. Remind me of that on my next birthday."

"It's so stupid. It isn't like you don't have a ton of experience. You had your own successful construction company, and even after you sold it, you were out helping on the In Step job sites all the time. Somebody's gotta see the value of that."

"Maybe I should take you with me on my next interview."

"Maybe you should." She nodded her head for emphasis.

It hurt her heart to see him looking defeated. That went so against his nature. No matter what the circumstances, he'd always held on to hope. He was the first one to lend a helping hand to a neighbor or a brother in Christ. He was the guy who came up with a million ideas when a problem needed solving. And when all else failed, he was a great one for making people laugh.

Now he looked like he might not ever laugh again.

They spent a short while looking over the menu and were ready when the waitress arrived. They both ordered their favorites. Comfort food and lots of it. She would need to walk an extra mile or two on her regular evening stroll.

After the waitress left their table, her dad said, "How's Hayley?"

Emma wished he hadn't asked. Talking about her sister wasn't likely to lighten his mood.

"I've left her a couple of messages," he added, "but she hasn't returned my calls."

"She's still pretty upset about losing the baby."

"She blames me for that."

She murmured something meant to sound like a denial, even though she knew he was right. Hayley did blame their dad. For the miscarriage, for the reporters, for the gossip, for it all.

"Yes, Emma, she does blame me."

"Well, if she does, she'll get over it. Give her some time. She'll come around. You'll see."

He lowered his gaze to his water glass that he turned slowly with his fingertips. His voice lowered. "Things aren't good between your mother and me either."

"Oh, Dad. I'm sorry."

"Well . . ." He drew in a breath as he sat straighter, his shoulders back and head up. "I didn't agree to meet you for lunch so I could depress you. Let's talk about something else, shall we? Didn't I hear something about Jason bringing home a puppy?"

Emma loved her dad. There wasn't anything she wouldn't do to lift his spirits. If talking about the puppy Jason had given her for Mother's Day would help, then that was what she would do.

For hours if necessary.

Twenty

I never should've agreed to this.

I slipped the pen into the top of the clipboard and returned the completed paperwork to the receptionist. The young woman smiled and said, "Donna will be with you shortly."

Donna O'Keefe was one of three professional counselors Susan had recommended to me. "You'll like her. She's a Christian like you and very down-to-earth."

I had no business seeing a counselor. Not with the hourly rate charged. Brad's medical coverage had ended when he began his unpaid leave, and COBRA was going to cost us an arm and a leg. But I'd finally faced the truth. I needed help. I was drowning in a sea of conflicting emotions. If I didn't want to counsel with someone at our church—and I didn't—then I would have to pay for someone's services.

I heard voices coming from the hallway. A moment later, two women entered the reception area. One was around my age, tall and slender, dressed in a business suit, a Blackberry held in her left hand. The other looked to be in her late fifties or early sixties. Her brown hair was streaked with gray, and she was what my mother called pleasantly plump. She wore a turquoise T-shirt-style top coupled with a long, flowing skirt.

I looked expectantly toward the younger of the two, but she walked past me and out the office door.

"Ms. Clarkson?"

I turned my gaze toward the older woman. "Yes."

She held out her hand. "I'm Donna O'Keefe. Why don't you come with me?"

I shook her hand, then rose and followed her down the narrow hallway. Nerves fluttered in my stomach. Maybe it would have been easier to talk to someone I knew rather than to a stranger. But at least Donna looked like a nice person. More like someone's grandmother than a college-educated professional with a half dozen initials after her name.

Her office had a modest-sized desk in one corner with a computer and a couple of bright-colored file folders on it. Two chairs, an upholstered rocker, and a sofa lined the walls, along with a bookcase and a number of children's toys.

"Would you like a beverage? We've got tea or coffee or a choice of sodas to offer."

"No, thank you. I'm fine."

She motioned toward the sofa, then she sat on the chair nearest the desk, the clipboard with my completed paperwork placed on her lap.

"Why don't you tell me about yourself."

"Where should I start?"

"Anywhere you wish." Her smile was both kind and patient.

I heard the soft ticking of the clock on the wall. "My husband is Brad Clarkson." I clenched and unclenched my hands. "Perhaps you've seen the news reports about him."

The kindness remained in her eyes. "Yes, I believe so."

"That's why I'm here."

Donna O'Keefe nodded once as she scribbled something on the paper on the clipboard. I wondered what she wrote. Perhaps it was better not to know.

I glanced toward the window, the lengthening silence making me uncomfortable, as if I was doing this all wrong. I wasn't used to talking about myself. Not about such private things.

I frowned. Susan said I had perfectionism and control issues. Was she right? I'd never thought so.

"Go on," Donna said.

Haltingly at first, I told her about the evening of the awards banquet, about Greta St. James and Nicole Schubert, about the troubles at In Step and Brad's decision to leave his position in an attempt to rescue the foundation from scandal and possible collapse.

But I didn't tell her how things were between Brad and me, about my fears and distrust, about how awful I felt that I had so little faith in him, how little faith I had in God to bring us through, about the anger that simmered below the surface of my emotions. I didn't tell her I was afraid my marriage might end, or that I felt helpless to do anything to stop it from happening, or that I sometimes wished it *would* end, which scared me even more. I didn't say that I felt like a failure, that I felt stupid and naive and ashamed and humiliated.

I couldn't. So I told her what I could, talking more about my daughters and their husbands, talking about the pain I felt over the lost grandchild, talking about my involvement at church, talking about anything except what mattered most. All the while, Donna watched, listened, nodded, and made an occasional sympathetic sound in her throat while she took notes.

When she glanced at her wristwatch, then set aside the pen, I knew the session was over. Funny, I wasn't ready to go. I wanted to say something that would make the past weeks disappear or change or become easier in some way. I wanted her to tell me what I could do to make that happen.

"I've got you down for the same time next week." Donna looked at her scheduling book. "Does that still work for you?"

I nodded, but inside I wondered if I would keep the appointment. I couldn't see that anything had been accomplished.

As if reading my mind, she said, "Don't worry, Katherine. These things take time to work through. Be patient."

I gave a half laugh. "I'm not a very patient person."

Another gentle smile—one that made me believe she might not think less of me were I to reveal the darker corners of my heart.

Maybe I would return next week.

Brad was mowing the backyard when I arrived home.

I hadn't told him that I'd made an appointment with a counselor. For that matter, the two of us rarely spoke to each other anymore. We'd been cocooned in silence since the day I discovered Nicole's name on the caller ID.

"*I can take everything else, Kat . . . But I can't take what's happening between us.*"

The defeat I'd heard in his voice when he spoke those words tugged at my heart even now. I didn't *want* to hurt him anymore than I wanted to *be* hurt.

Or maybe I *did* want to hurt him. Maybe I wanted to see him suffer. I blamed him for our current troubles, and we both knew it.

I stood for a short while at the kitchen window, watching

Brad push the mower from one end of the yard to the other. He'd been out looking for work when I left to see the counselor. I hoped he wouldn't ask where I'd been.

The growl of the mower fell silent. An instant later I realized he stood near the patio, staring at me through the window. After a few moments, he walked across the concrete, removed his shoes, and opened the back door, stepping inside in his stocking feet.

"Have you been home long?" he asked.

"Not long."

He pointed toward the answering machine. "You've got a couple of messages from gals in your Bible study group."

I nodded. "I'll listen to them later."

At least one woman from my study group had called me every day since this nightmare began. After canceling our regular meeting on the night of Nicole's *Our View* interview, I'd made the decision to begin our group's summer break several weeks earlier than other years. I was too emotionally overwhelmed to continue with it. Thankfully, they'd understood.

"We're praying for you," were words I'd heard daily ever since.

"I've got good news," Brad said, intruding on my thoughts. "I found work. I start tomorrow. It's temporary but the pay is fair."

"What sort of work?"

"Framing. Swinging the old hammer." He mimed the action. "The boss thought he could use me for about a month."

A month. That wasn't long.

"I'll keep looking for a permanent position in my off-hours."

Our savings account balance was well below what it needed to be, and our retirement accounts were almost a joke. Our financial advisor had told us repeatedly that we needed to be more disciplined about setting aside money for emergencies. Brad would agree and promise to be better about saving. Then he would hear about an individual who needed financial help or about another good cause in need. And the money would be gone.

I swallowed a sigh. "Have you heard anything from Stan about the AG's investigation? If they clear you . . ." I let the sentence go unfinished.

Brad shook his head. "No word yet. And even if that's cleared up soon, the . . . other matter is unresolved."

Unresolved. Meaning the board still might not reinstate him because of Nicole. At least not any time soon.

"Will we have enough money to see us through?" I asked.

"God will provide, Kat."

"God will provide." Brad said those words often. He believed them. Did I?

Bad things happened to good people. I knew that. Even the Bible said "when" instead of "if." But I'd believed we were exempt. After all, we'd devoted our lives to God's service. We shouldn't have to walk through the fire or pass through the waters. Should we?

It isn't fair.

I heard the whine in my thoughts.

I'm sure God heard it too.

Twenty-one

I WAS IN THE GROCERY STORE, IN THE CANNED FRUITS AND vegetables aisle, when I came face-to-face with Nicole Schubert. Our gazes collided, and we froze, like wild animals caught in a rifle's crosshairs.

Conflicting impulses warred within me. I wanted to whirl about and run from the store. I wanted to slam my grocery cart into her, causing her pain, maybe breaking something.

I did neither.

"Katherine," she said at last.

I wouldn't dignify her greeting with a reply.

"I know you must be hurt, finding out this way."

"Don't speak to me." My words were barely audible. "Don't you *dare* speak to me."

"I never meant to hurt you. It just happened. I couldn't—"

I grabbed my purse from the cart, turned on my heel, and headed for the exit. I'd reached my car before I realized Nicole had followed me outside. I pressed the remote to unlock the door. *Hurry. Hurry. Hurry.*

"Katherine, wait. We should talk."

I whirled around, blinded with sudden rage. "Don't say another word. Leave me alone."

"Don't you want to hear my side of the story?"

"No." The word was squeezed through gritted teeth. "I don't want to hear anything you have to say."

"I can't help it that I fell in love with Brad."

Clichéd though it might be, I wanted to scratch her eyes out.

"I'll bet he denies the affair, doesn't he? I'll bet he swears he's innocent."

In my peripheral vision, I saw people stopping in the parking lot, staring at us—the betrayed wife and her husband's mistress. Thanks to the local news, our faces were known to thousands of strangers.

Nicole took a step closer to me. "He should have kept the promises he made me. None of this had to happen this way. No one else needed to become involved." She paused and her eyes widened. "I don't believe it. You're going to stand by him, aren't you?"

I wasn't about to give her the satisfaction of a reply. Or maybe I didn't know what to say. Was I going to stand by him?

"Katherine, you're a bigger fool than I thought."

Her words were like a slap. They sent me spinning toward my car. I yanked open the door and got in. Hand shaking, I managed—after two failed attempts—to fit the key into the ignition switch. When I looked up again, Nicole was gone.

The shaking spread throughout my body. Drawing in a breath, I hit the steering wheel with the balls of my hands. Once. Twice. Again. A sound rose up from that spot just above the breastbone and tore itself from my throat. Part groan. Part squeal.

Why? I want to know why!

It was a good five to ten minutes before I felt under control again, enough to start the engine and leave the grocery store's parking lot. As I drove toward home, I heard voices from the past weeks replaying in my mind.

"Listen to me." Emma. *"She's lying. Anyone who knows Dad the way we do won't give credence to what she says."*

Hayley. *"Mom, if you think Dad was unfaithful, you don't have to stay with him. You can come stay with me and Steve until you get things sorted out."*

Susan. *"I'm never surprised when a man strays. I guess I'm more surprised when they don't."*

Nicole. *"I'll bet he denies the affair, doesn't he? I'll bet he swears he's innocent."*

Brad. *"It isn't true, Kat."*

Nicole. *"Katherine, you're a bigger fool than I thought."*

Brad. *"I was never unfaithful. I swear it."*

Nicole. *"You're a bigger fool than I thought."*

A bigger fool . . . a bigger fool . . . a bigger fool . . .

"It isn't true, Kat."

Who could find the truth in all the chaos that had become my life?

I stood in the middle of the master bedroom, staring at the queen-sized four-poster bed with its gold-colored duvet and assortment of pillows in various shades of brown.

When we moved into this house, we'd purchased a king-sized mattress and bed frame. After all, with a bedroom as spacious as this one, we could have a large bed without it seeming crowded or cramped. But it wasn't long—at most six or eight months—before Brad declared he didn't like it. The bed was too big, not conducive to snuggling, and he loved to snuggle before we drifted off to sleep each night.

We hadn't done any snuggling recently. Not since the night when my defenses were down and I allowed myself to take comfort in his arms, to believe in his love. A part of me ached to be held by him still. A part of me longed for his sweet kisses, for his tender caresses.

But I wanted nothing to do with that part of me. Not when I imagined him holding Nicole, caressing Nicole, kissing Nicole . . . perhaps even loving Nicole.

I moved to the dresser, opened the top drawer, and began pulling out clothes and piling them on the bed. The top drawer, the next, and the next, until all were empty. Then I gathered as much as I could into my arms and carried it down the hall to Emma's old bedroom. By the time Brad came home from his first day at his new job, there wasn't a trace of me left in the master bedroom or the master bath. It took him a while to find me in the smaller bedroom at the end of the hall.

"Kat? What are you doing in here?"

I rose from the edge of the bed. "I . . . I thought it would be better if I stayed in a separate room."

His gaze flickered to the twin bed, then back to me. "Why would it be better?"

"Because I . . . I'm not sleeping very well at night. I thought I might . . . sleep better alone."

"I see."

I wanted to feel victorious in some small way. I wanted to be glad that I had the upper hand, that I'd taken control of the situation and made decisions for myself.

But there was no victory, no gladness.

"For how long?" he asked.

I ignored the question, saying instead, "I saw Nicole at the grocery store today."

"Is that what this is about?"

"She called me a fool."

"Kat—"

"Maybe she's right. Maybe I am a fool." I clenched my hands at my sides. "I feel like one."

He stared at me a long while in silence. Then, without another word, he walked away.

I crossed to the door and closed it, turned around and leaned my back against it.

This room had changed little since Emma left home two years before. The tassel from her high school academic cap hung over the mirror of the dressing table that had belonged to my grandmother. Framed photographs that Emma had taken as part of a photography class in her junior year covered a good section of one wall. The quilted spread on the twin bed was made from a hideous tie-dyed fabric she had found in a second-hand store.

I wasn't going to like staying in here. The air felt too still, the walls too close.

I should have moved *his* things out of our room. *He* should be the one who had to move, not me. It shouldn't have to be me.

Twenty-two

I AWAKENED MY FIRST MORNING IN MY NEW ROOM TO THE scent of bacon frying. Saturday. Brad was cooking breakfast. Perhaps one of his omelets. The table would be set, the newspaper waiting for us to read to one another.

I pulled the pillow over my face, telling myself I wasn't hungry. I didn't want to go downstairs. I didn't want to sit across the table from Brad. I didn't. I really didn't.

Only I did.

How does a person fall out of love? It would make things so much easier if I didn't care about Brad. Hate would be even better. I wanted to hate him. If I hated him, I could . . .

Leave?

I drew the pillow down from my face, hugging it to my chest while I stared at the ceiling.

Did I want to leave? I'd never lived alone. Not ever. I'd gone from my mother's home to a year or so of sharing an apartment with a roommate to marriage. Would I be able to manage on my own or would I fall flat on my face? Hayley had said I could stay with her and Steve. I wouldn't have to be alone. Not right away. Not until I found work. Not until I was financially able.

But do I want to go?

If Brad was innocent, as he claimed to be—

A knock on the door. "Kat, breakfast is ready."

I could say I wasn't hungry. I could tell him to eat without me. I said, "I'll be down in a minute." I sat up on the edge of the bed, brushing my hair back from my face and hooking it behind my ears.

Lord, are You there? I'm lost and confused. I don't know how to pray. I don't hear Your voice and can't seem to find Your answers.

I stepped toward the dressing table, staring at my reflection in the mirror as I drew close. My complexion seemed sallow. My hair was stringy and lifeless, my eyes ringed in shadows that bespoke my sleepless nights. I took my hairbrush from the top of the vanity and ran its bristles down the length of my hair.

What should I do?

I used to tell the women in my Bible study that God caused

or allowed people and circumstances to enter their lives out of love in order to refine them, to make them more like Jesus. Did I still believe it? I didn't feel more refined or Christlike. Anything but. And bringing Nicole into our lives did not seem a loving thing to do.

"Katherine, you're a bigger fool than I thought."

"Shut up," I whispered. "Leave me alone."

This must be how madness began. With telling the voices in one's head to shut up.

I put the brush on the vanity, turned, and left the bedroom.

Brad had set the table with our everyday dishes and silverware. Flowers, cut from our garden, were arranged in a vase in the center of the table. A tall pitcher of orange juice waited near my place setting, along with a mug of steaming coffee.

I looked toward Brad as I entered the kitchen but lowered my gaze when I found him watching me.

Distant strangers. That's what we'd become. We shared a home but all intimacy between us was gone.

Without a word, I took my seat and Brad served me. He'd made my favorite omelet—crumbled bacon, shredded hash browns, chopped onions and green peppers, and plenty of cheddar cheese.

Was he trying to curry favor?

Despite thinking I wasn't hungry, I ate. First one small bite, and then another and another until my plate was clean.

If Brad dared say anything about my healthy appetite, so help me, I'd smack him.

But he didn't even notice. His attention was on the newspaper, his expression grave.

"There's more about us in the paper today," he said.

My stomach plummeted. "More?"

"Do you want to read it?"

"No." I shook my head. "You tell me what it says. And . . . make it brief."

Brad glanced down at the folded newspaper in his right hand. "It begins with a quote from Stan saying the AG review is still in progress and that they are not expecting to do a more extensive investigation." He glanced at me, then back at the paper. "Stan says that I'm pursuing all avenues in order to clear my name of the false accusations made against me."

I moved crumbs around my plate with a fork. "Why don't they let the matter drop? We're not really news anymore."

"Sure we are. Or at least I am. I will be as long as there's a chance I'll be proven guilty. I will be as long as there's a hope a Christian could take a hard fall."

He was right, and I knew it.

He continued with his summation of the article: "It goes on to say that we've been married close to twenty-five years and quotes one of our unnamed neighbors as saying that from all appearances, it seemed to be a good marriage."

Which neighbor, I wondered, picturing them in my head.

"There's a little about my parents and your mom," Brad continued, "and it mentions we have two married daughters. There's some about our involvement with our church and the community, too."

None of that seemed very interesting. Nothing scandalous. In fact, just the opposite. Hardly worth mentioning.

"The rest is about Nicole."

Oh, how I'd come to hate that name.

"What does it say?" I asked in a whisper.

"It appears she's had affairs with two married men in the past. Both of them were her employers." He looked up again. "I believe that's meant to make me look all the more guilty."

"It does." I didn't realize I'd said the words aloud until I saw him flinch.

He set the newspaper on the table and rose from his chair. After a moment's hesitation while he looked at me—I suppose waiting for me to say something more—he went to the sink and began rinsing dishes and cookware. But then he stopped. The skillet clattered into the sink. The noise caused me to twist on my chair to look behind me.

"What are we going to do, Kat?"

"I don't know what you mean." But I did.

"I can proclaim my innocence from now to eternity, and it still isn't going to make a difference. It's much easier to prove that something happened than it is to prove something *didn't* happen. Did you know that? I've talked to Stan about suing Nicole for slander, but I don't have peace about going that route. It could make things worse."

How?

"Kat, I don't have proof to give you or anyone else. I only have my word. When Nicole worked for In Step, I had private business meetings with her regarding the financial aspects of the foundation. I had lunch with her, the two of us, in public restaurants. I even drove her home a couple of different times when she had car trouble. But I was never inside her house except when you were with me. I never took her to a motel. I never touched her inappropriately." He drew a breath. "But like I said, those are just my words. They aren't proof of what didn't happen."

I shook my head.

"If you want me to say I'm sorry, I'll say it. I'm sorry for anything I ever did that caused you to doubt me. I'm sorry for any time you felt neglected or abandoned, any time I've hurt you because I was thoughtless or clueless."

"Brad—"

He swore as he wadded the dishcloth into a ball and tossed it into the sink. "You know what Nicole wants out of all this?"

A chill shivered up my spine. "No."

"She doesn't want me. She wants to ruin us. I didn't understand that at first, but I do now. She wants to ruin you and me. And she may accomplish it. Is that what you want, too?"

No.

Brad circumvented the table and went to stand at the kitchen window. His voice was softer when he spoke again. "I can only do so much. I love you. I've never cheated on you. I want us to make it. But if you want out . . ."

The unspoken hung in the air between us. I couldn't breathe. *If you want out . . .*

If I wanted a divorce. That's what he meant. If I wanted a divorce.

But divorce wasn't supposed to happen to women like me. I'd made a good home for my husband, wasn't a nag, never berated him. I'd tried to be his helpmeet, his biggest cheerleader, a constant source of support, willing to listen when he needed a sounding board, offering advice when he asked for it. I'd read books found in the Christian Living section of the bookstore—ones that encouraged me to pray for my husband, books that helped me understand the different ways men and women communicate, the different ways we think, even the different ways we express love. I'd been a good steward of my household. I'd taken care of my body, working out at the gym several days a week, eating the right foods, taking my vitamins. I'd been a good mother to our daughters and brought them up to love the Lord and honor their parents.

I wasn't supposed to find my life ripped to shreds in an instant. I wasn't supposed to face the specter of divorce.

Brad faced me again, the light from the window casting a yellow silhouette around him. "What is it you want, Kat?"

"I want it all to go away. I want it not to be happening."

"You won't get that wish."

I didn't reply.

"Shall I leave? Do you want me to move out?"

My stomach hurt. Not just a sick feeling. A sharp pain. "I don't know." I bent forward, pressing crossed arms against my stomach. "I . . . I'm confused. I'm hurt. I don't know what to think or feel. I don't know what I want."

He gave me no quarter. "You need to decide." He ran his fingers through his hair. "We can't go on like this much longer. Neither one of us."

I know. I know.

He drew in a deep breath, his shoulders rising and falling with the effort. "I'm going to get dressed and go out for a while, before I say something I'll regret."

I didn't try to stop him. I couldn't. I had nothing to say.

Emma arrived a little after one o'clock. When I opened the door for her, I could tell she was ready to blow.

"Dad came over this morning. He's with Jason now."

I turned and walked down the hall.

"Mom, what's wrong with you?"

"Nothing is wrong with me."

"Dad thinks you might ask him to move out."

I sank onto my chair in the family room.

"He said you're sleeping in my old room."

I wished he hadn't told her that.

"You've got to snap out of this. Think about what you're doing."

"Emma, all I *do* is think about it. I can't go out of the house without having people stare at me or running into people I don't want to see." I pictured Nicole in the grocery aisle. "So here I stay, most of the day, thinking about what the papers have said and what the TV reporters have said and what strangers on the Internet have said." I waved my hands in the air. "How am I supposed to react to all of that? Am I supposed to ignore what they're saying about your father?" *What Nicole says about him.*

"Yes." Her answer was firm. "If you love him, yes."

What did she know? She was young and innocent. She couldn't begin to understand the things I felt. She hadn't seen herself on the nightly news or read about her husband in the paper. She hadn't felt people staring at her wherever she went.

"You've got to give him a chance, Mom."

"Would you feel the same way if it was Jason who had an affair?"

"Dad *didn't* have an affair."

"All right then. Was *accused* of having an affair."

"I'd believe Jason."

"Would you?" I released a heavy sigh. "Don't be too sure. It's different when it happens to you."

"Do you want a divorce? Is that what you're after?"

There was that sharp pain in my stomach again, like it was being ripped in two.

"Do you?"

I whispered my answer. "No."

It was true. I didn't want my marriage to end. I didn't want to be a divorced woman. Divorce wasn't an option for me. For other women, perhaps, but not for me. God hated divorce and so would I. I didn't want others to look at me and judge me a failure. I didn't want God to judge me a failure either.

Emma said, "If that's true—if you don't want a divorce—you're going to have to change what you're doing. You can't treat Dad like a pariah in his own home. You can't live in this house like a couple of strangers."

I bristled. "I don't think it's your place to tell me what I should or should not do."

"Why not? I'm your daughter."

"And I'm your mother. You're supposed to honor me."

Disdain filled her eyes. "The way you're honoring your husband?" She spun about and disappeared down the hall. Moments later, I heard the front door slam in her wake.

It felt as if all the oxygen in the house went with Emma. I struggled to draw breath as silence closed in around me.

Nicole

NICOLE WAS FRUSTRATED, EVEN A LITTLE BORED. AN entire month had passed since she made her first telephone call to Greta St. James at Channel 5, suggesting Brad Clarkson wasn't all the newspaper had made him out to be. It was almost as long since she called the office of the attorney general, setting in motion the financial review at In Step.

Like most government agencies, the AG seemed content to move at a snail's pace. Not that she expected them to find anything damaging. As the former CFO, she knew the foundation's financial records were in order. Her greatest regret was that she hadn't taken the time to make some intentional errors before she quit. It wouldn't have been too difficult to change things enough to give Brad headaches for months to come.

If only she hadn't lost her temper . . .

At least she could take satisfaction in the news that Brad was no longer at the helm of the foundation. She knew how much he loved that place. He loved remodeling dilapidated houses, turning them into something special, then handing the keys to the new owners, people who, without In Step's help, would probably never own a home of their own. It had to hurt him, not being involved in that work any longer.

And then there was Katherine, little Miss Susie Homemaker. Sweet enough to make a person gag. Well, she hadn't been so sweet yesterday at the store. She'd run like a scared rabbit.

Yet even that wasn't enough to appease Nicole, not as long as Katherine stayed with Brad. Nicole wanted him left with nothing. She wanted him alone and miserable. She wanted him to hurt. She wanted him rejected by the world. She hoped he lost that smile of his forever.

Most of all, she hoped he choked on his so-called Christian principles.

Twenty-three

IT WAS ALMOST DARK WHEN BRAD RETURNED HOME. I was
on the patio, wrapped in a bulky sweater against the early evening
chill. He didn't call my name when he entered the house. Neither
did I call out to him, wasn't sure he cared to know where I was.
But eventually he joined me in the gathering darkness.

He sat in the padded chair to my right. "Emma said she came
to see you."

"Yes, she was here."

"She said you don't want me to move out. Is that true?
Because when I left this morning, I thought—"

"It's true. I . . . I want you to stay."

"And you don't want a divorce."

"No."

Silence, then, "That's good."

I pulled the sweater tighter about me, my arms folded over my chest.

"It's a place to start, Kat. We can work our way back from there."

I wasn't so sure I agreed. It didn't feel like a starting point. It felt like a big, black, bottomless hole. It felt hopeless.

"Are you going to church in the morning?"

I drew in a deep breath, answering on the exhale, "Yes."

I didn't want to go, wasn't ready to face the curious glances, the whispers hidden behind raised hands, not even the words of encouragement from friends. But I'd already missed three Sundays in a row. I'd already decided that our women's Bible study would begin its summer break a month earlier than usual. People had to be wondering about me. I didn't want them wondering, speculating, gossiping.

For appearances' sake, if nothing more, I needed to go to church. I needed to walk in at Brad's side and smile and tell people that we were fine, that I was fine.

I won't let on how things really are. I won't give her the satisfaction.

Her.

Nicole.

"Don't you want to hear my side of the story?"

No, I didn't. I didn't want to hear anything from her or about her ever again. When I remembered how she'd pretended to be my friend . . .

"I'll bet he denies the affair, doesn't he? I'll bet he swears he's innocent."

I cast a sideways glance at Brad. He was hidden in the shadows of nightfall, but after so many years, I didn't need light to see him. I knew every plane and angle of his face. I'd loved every plane and angle. I'd loved him.

"You're going to stand by him, aren't you?"

Was staying *with* him the same thing as standing *by* him? I thought not. But it was the best I could do for now.

"You're a bigger fool than I thought."

Nicole thought me a fool. She must have always thought me a fool. She'd waltzed into my home, tried to steal my husband from under my nose, and I hadn't suspected a thing. Not a thing.

A soft breeze whispered across the patio, and I realized my cheeks were damp with tears.

I was sick of tears.

Emma

Emma called Hayley to let her know the latest about their parents, hoping between the two of them that they could come up with some way to help.

"Stay out of it," Hayley said. "Mom shouldn't even stay at the house. She should move out and file for divorce. I already told her she could come live with me and Steve for as long as she needs."

"Divorce? Hayley, how can you say that? Divorce isn't the answer."

"Sometimes it is. I wouldn't stay with Steve if he cheated on me. Not for a single day. Why should Mom stay with Dad?"

"There's no proof that he cheated. He says he didn't. We owe it to him to believe him."

Hayley made a scoffing sound in her throat.

"Nicole Schubert is *lying*. Why are you so determined to believe the worst about Dad?"

"Because I'm more realistic than you are. If an attractive woman comes on to a man, we all know what happens."

"That sounds like something Susan Bales would say." Emma's hand shook as she held the phone against her ear. "And it isn't true. Dad wouldn't cheat. Jason wouldn't cheat."

"Sure they wouldn't." Her voice was hard with sarcasm. "You're almost as naive as Mom. You know that?"

Their conversation unraveled into raised voices, hurtful words tossed back and forth, and finally, Hayley slammed down the phone, ending the connection.

Emma stayed seated on the chair in the kitchen, her breathing fast and shallow, the words they'd said to each other repeating in her head. How, she wondered, had such a well-intentioned phone call gone so wrong so fast? They'd had some crazy fights through the years, but this was about their parents. They should be united, not quarreling.

Maybe Hayley's anger had more to do with losing the baby than it did about their dad. Maybe her hormones were all out of whack.

Still . . .

Jason poked his head into the room. "Is it safe to come in yet or are bullets still flying?"

Emma burst into tears.

"Hey, babe. I'm sorry." He hurried to her and drew her up from the chair and into his arms. "I shouldn't have kidded around like that. I'm sorry."

"It . . . isn't . . . you." Sniff. "I . . . I just . . . don't know . . . why she has . . . has to be . . . like that."

He caressed her hair with one hand, held her close with the other. "You know Hayley. When she thinks she's right, it's her way or the highway."

"She thinks all men will cheat if a woman is willing."

"She's wrong about that. Not all men. I wouldn't, and I don't think your dad would either."

Emma sniffed. "Hayley wants Mom to get a divorce, and she's mad at her for not leaving Dad already."

"We'll pray it doesn't come to that."

Emma lifted her head from her husband's chest so she could look him in the eyes. "Do you think it will?"

"No." He kissed the tip of her nose. "I don't think it will."

She released a deep breath. "Hayley blames Dad for her losing the baby because of that reporter. But she hadn't been feeling well even before that happened. She told me so."

"I know."

"It wasn't his fault, but I'm not sure she'll ever admit it."

Jason cupped her chin with his hand as he leaned in. "Don't worry about tomorrow. Today has enough trouble of its own.

Give God some time to work. He's got plans we don't know anything about. You'll see."

She gave him a tremulous smile. "I love you."

"Love you back."

Twenty-four

GOING TO CHURCH THAT SUNDAY WAS BOTH BETTER AND worse than I'd anticipated.

Friends expressed how good it was to see me again and murmured those expected words of encouragement, saying they were praying for us and that they knew the truth would come out. Some took my hand and squeezed my fingers, gestures of love and comfort. I received several warm hugs from women who'd attended my Bible study through the years. Likewise, there were men extending hands of friendship to Brad.

But there were also those who stared and whispered. I knew what they thought. I could guess what they said. I was aware of them even when I didn't look around.

We didn't sit in our usual place. That was my choice. As soon as we entered the sanctuary, I slipped into the back row. Brad gave me a questioning glance, but I ignored him. After a moment, he sat beside me. I leaned toward the opposite side of my chair, ensuring our shoulders wouldn't touch.

Help me, Lord.

If ever I'd come to church needing to hear from God, it was today. I needed Him to tell me what to do, what to say, where to go, how to survive until my world was set to right again.

It would be set to right again, wouldn't it?

Desert experiences. I'd heard people talk about them throughout my Christian walk, but I hadn't understood what they meant until now. Not only was the desert hot and dry, it was barren and lonely. God was absent in the desert place.

Where are You?

The worship team began singing an up-tempo song. Out of habit, I stood, but there was no melody in my heart, no words of praise in my mouth. The desert had dried me to dust.

It's too hard, God. You're asking too much. Rescue me.

Eyes closed, I admitted an unpleasant truth that I'd done my best to ignore for weeks: my faith was not what I'd thought it was. It wasn't strong and victorious. It wasn't unshakeable. It hadn't been tested. Perhaps God had spared me the testing because He knew how utterly I would fail, the way I was failing now.

Wasn't a faltering marriage enough without a faltering faith too?

Silence was our partner as we drove home an hour and a half later. In the past, this was when Brad would share something specific from the sermon that had challenged or enlightened him. But today he was quiet. Perhaps he'd heard no more of the service than I had.

I glanced toward him. His brow was furrowed, eyes squinting against the sunlight. What was he thinking? I wondered.

There was a time, not long before, when I would have ventured to guess his thoughts. I'd believed he was an open book to me, his wife. How wrong could a woman be? Even if he hadn't been unfaithful, as he insisted, he'd still kept secrets.

I turned my head to look out the window at the passing street scene. Tidy houses in established neighborhoods. Tall, leafy trees casting shadows over rooftops. Lawns in deep shades of green, many of them freshly mown. Flowers abloom around foundations and along walkways. I'd paid little attention to my yard this spring. Had weeds overtaken my flower gardens?

"Hayley and Steve weren't in church today," Brad said, breaking the silence.

I turned from the window to look at him.

His gaze remained on the street. "Have you talked to either of them in the last few days?"

"No. I left a message for Hayley on her voice mail, but I haven't heard back."

"She hasn't returned my calls either." He paused, then said, "I'm worried about her."

I was worried too. Hayley was depressed about the baby and angry with her father and me. Because of her anger I hadn't been allowed to mourn with her over the grandchild I would never hold, the child she would never see grow up. I pushed the switch to lower my window, needing fresh air on my face. I was grateful to see we were on our street now. We would be home soon. I wanted out of the car, out of the thick, uncomfortable silence that had returned to sit between us.

Secrets and silence. That's what my life had become.

Twenty-five

MUSIC DRIFTED FROM THE PORTABLE CD PLAYER AS I knelt beside my rose bushes, perspiration trickling down the sides of my face. The heat of early afternoon felt more like midsummer than the middle of May. I raised my shoulders, one at a time, and wiped away the dampness on the short sleeves of my shirt.

Just a little more weeding, I thought, and I would take a short break. A tall glass of iced tea in the shade of the covered patio sounded ideal right about then.

A car pulled into the driveway, and I turned to see who it was—friend or foe. Annabeth Sorenson. Friend.

She waved as she got out of her car. "Hi, Katherine."

"Hi, Annabeth." I rose to my feet.

"I hope you don't mind my dropping by like this."

"Of course not."

"I saw you at church yesterday, but you left before I got a chance to talk to you."

I offered a brief smile as she walked toward me but gave no explanation for our quick departure.

Her eyes studied me. "How are you doing?"

"Okay."

"Really?"

I wasn't a very good liar. "Well enough."

"Can I intrude upon your gardening?" She motioned toward the rose bushes. "I promise not to stay long."

"I was about to take a break anyway. Come inside, and I'll pour us both a glass of iced tea."

"Thanks. That sounds wonderful. I can't believe how warm it is, and summer hasn't even begun yet."

I turned off the CD player on my way into the house, Annabeth following close behind. We went into the kitchen, and she sat on a chair at the table while I took two tall glasses from the cupboard, dropped in a few ice cubes, and filled them with tea from the pitcher in the refrigerator. I took the glasses to the table, then made a second trip for the sugar bowl and a saucer of sliced lemons.

Before I sat down across from her, I asked, "Would you like milk or artificial sweetener? I have both."

"No." She waved her hand. "This is perfect. Really. I didn't come over to have you wait on me."

I sat across from her.

"I've been worried about you, Katherine."

I sipped my tea.

"I learned last week from Martha Egbert that you've canceled your Bible study."

I shook my head. My shoulders tightened. "Not canceled, Annabeth. I decided to begin our summer break earlier than usual. We'll resume again in the fall."

"Oh, dear." She leaned against the back of her chair. "I didn't mean to sound like I disapproved of your decision. I don't. It's just . . . It's just I think you need these women to gather around you right now. Even if they only came over to pray for you each week."

Did my smile look as forced as it felt?

"You and Brad are so dear to us, Katherine."

"You and Mike are dear to us too." I focused my eyes on the ice cubes floating in my tea.

"Naturally, Mike hasn't told me anything Brad's shared in their sessions together, but I know it isn't easy for a man to go through something like this."

Sessions together?

Why that surprised me I couldn't say. It was the most natural thing in the world for a man to meet with his pastor, especially in times of trouble. And my husband was without a doubt in trouble. Still, it did surprise me that he'd met with Mike. He hadn't mentioned it even once, but according to Annabeth, there had been multiple sessions. And yet I knew nothing.

Secrets. More secrets between us.

"It can't be easy for you either." Annabeth reached across the table and touched the back of my hand. "Your church family wants to help carry the burden in whatever way we can. God doesn't mean for us to go it alone in this life. Promise me you won't do that."

I released a shudder of air. "I promise, Annabeth. But really, we're doing fine. Our attorney told us last week that the AG should be nearing a decision in the next week or two. He doesn't anticipate the investigation will go any further."

"Yes, I read that in Saturday's paper. That's good news."

I continued as if she hadn't spoken. "Brad is working again so we don't have any financial concerns." That was stretching the truth a bit. "I'm sure the whole mess will blow over soon."

If she didn't believe me, she was gracious enough not to say it aloud. She allowed me to stay wrapped in the tatters of my dignity.

Over the next half hour, she asked after Hayley and Emma and their husbands, shared some about an upcoming mission trip to Africa, and finally offered to pray for me. When she finished, I walked with her to the door and thanked her for coming. She held my hand and kissed my cheek, told me again how loved I was, then said good-bye and walked to her car.

I cast a quick glance at the CD player on the sidewalk and the garden trowel waiting for me near the rose bushes. But I was exhausted. All I wanted to do was lie down and sleep.

You're turning into a slug.

I returned to the kitchen for a quick cleanup and was almost finished when the phone rang. Caller ID showed an unfamiliar number and no name. I almost let it go to the machine, then at the last moment picked up.

"Hello."

"Is this Mrs. Clarkson?"

"Yes."

"I'm Doug Norton, the foreman on the job your husband's working."

"Yes?"

"There's been an accident on the site. Brad's on his way to the hospital."

I sank onto a chair, nearly missing it. I grabbed for the edge of the seat to keep myself from toppling to the floor. "What happened? Is he—"

"He's not in any danger, I don't think. But he's kinda busted up. His leg's broke for sure."

A breath escaped me.

"They took him to St. Alphonsus 'cause it was closest. If you need somebody to come get you, we can—"

"Thank you, but I have a car. I'll leave right away." I hung up without saying good-bye.

An accident. A broken leg. *"Busted up."*

I grabbed my purse and raced to my car. I forgot about my bedraggled appearance—untidy hair and jeans with knees that were dirt and grass stained—until I was halfway to the hospital. By then it was too late to turn back.

I parked in the ER lot and rushed in through the large automatic doors, my heart pumping. The clerk behind the admitting desk looked at me with a practiced gaze that said she'd seen countless people come through those doors in similar states of dishevelment, fear, and confusion.

"I'm looking for my husband, Brad Clarkson. He . . . he was in an accident and they were bringing him here. Has he arrived? Is he all right?"

"Why don't you sit down while I check?" She motioned toward the chair beside her desk. "What did you say his name is?"

"Brad Clarkson."

"Was it an automobile accident?"

"No. He was at work." I turned anxious eyes toward the doors leading into the emergency room area.

"Was he brought in by ambulance?"

I nodded, then shook my head. "I don't know. The man who called didn't say. I assumed . . ."

"It's okay. Just sit tight. He isn't showing on my screen yet, but that doesn't mean he isn't here. I'll go check and let you know."

I couldn't obey her instructions to sit tight. The instant she disappeared into a neighboring room, I got up and began to pace, walking toward the entry doors to the ER, then back toward the admitting area. Back and forth. Back and forth.

"Mrs. Clarkson?"

I spun around at my name. "Yes."

"Your husband is here. They've taken him to X-ray, but he'll be back soon. If you'd come with me, I'll take you to the examination room. You can wait for him there."

I nodded and fell into step behind her as she led me through the labyrinth that made up the ER. Finally she stopped outside a room filled with all the usual hospital paraphernalia.

"Right in here," the clerk said.

I nodded again and took a step forward. There was no bed in the room, but I saw some clothes on the floor. Brad's clothes. A brown cotton shirt, faded Levis, and work boots. The shirt was splattered with blood, and there was more blood on the jeans and the gray linoleum floor.

The clerk said something, but I couldn't make sense of it. Her voice sounded like it came through a tunnel. I turned my head as the walls waved and shivered and lights exploded in my head, then dimmed.

"Mrs. Clarkson!"

The floor rose up to meet me, and after that, nothing.

Twenty-six

SOMETHING PUNGENT STUNG MY NOSTRILS. I JERKED MY head to the side and inhaled through my mouth.

"Mrs. Clarkson."

I opened my eyes. Bright lights everywhere. White. Lots and lots of white. Where was I?

"There we go. You gave us a scare, Mrs. Clarkson. Took ten years off poor Carol's life. Let's get you up off the floor, shall we?"

"What happened?"

The hospital. Brad. The admitting clerk. But the woman who knelt beside me wasn't the same one who'd led me into the ER. This woman wore hospital scrubs, the top in a multicolored-flowered pattern, and had a stethoscope around her neck. She must be a nurse.

She slipped an arm beneath my back and with her other hand grasped my elbow and eased me up to a sitting position. "Take a deep breath. How are you feeling?"

"Okay." The room wobbled, then steadied. "I'm fine. What happened?"

"You fainted."

"Fainted? I've never fainted in my life."

She didn't bother to argue with me. Something in her expression—probably the way she fought to keep from smiling—said she'd heard similar protests before. "Are you ready to stand?"

"Yes."

She was strong. I'd give her that. A good thing, too, because, once I was up, I found I wasn't as steady on my feet as I thought I'd be. With an arm around my back and a firm grip on my elbow, she ushered me into the exam room and eased me onto the lone chair. My gaze drifted to the clothes on the floor nearby.

"Easy there." She brought the smelling salts near my nose again.

I gasped and turned my head away. "Please. No more."

This time she smiled. "I think you'll be all right now." She straightened away from me. "Is this your first time to the ER?"

I shook my head.

"Kids? That's often what brings people to the ER."

I nodded. "Two daughters. But they're grown now."

"Really? You look too young to have grown children."

She was being kind. I knew I must look a fright.

"Thanks," I said. Another glance at the clothes on the floor. "Can you tell me what's happened to my husband? All I know is he got injured at work."

The nurse filled a Dixie cup with water from the sink and handed it to me. "Let me see if the doctor is able to talk to you. You just sit there and don't move. You still look a bit pale."

I felt pale—and more than a little embarrassed. I'd seen blood before. Like the nurse said, I had kids. When Hayley was eleven, she rode her bike into a parked car. Her head bled like a stuck pig, and it took over ten stitches to close the gap in her scalp. At the age of seven, Emma climbed onto the kitchen counter to get something off the top shelf of the cupboard. She slipped and fell, cutting the underside of her chin and blackening her eye. I'd forgotten how many stitches she needed.

This wasn't Brad's only trip to the ER either. He'd worked in construction his entire adult life. He'd experienced his share of mishaps and shed his share of blood because of them.

I hadn't fainted over any of those previous calamities, whether major or minor. I'd often been the person in charge of stopping the bleeding and taking the injured party to the near-est clinic or hospital. I knew how to answer all the questions from the admitting clerk while still tending to a crying child. I was not some sort of swooning airhead.

Or at least, I didn't used to be.

I leaned over and picked up the shirt, wrapping my fingers in the fabric as I lifted it to my face and breathed in.

Let him be okay, God. No matter what I've—

I heard laughter in the hallway. A moment later, a gurney was wheeled into view, Brad lying on the bed. His face was swollen, so much so that for a second I thought it wasn't him after all. But then he saw me and raised his left hand in acknowledgment before they turned the gurney around and rolled it headfirst into the examination room.

I clutched his shirt to my chest.

"I'm okay, Kat," he said when he could see me again.

He didn't look okay. He looked dreadful.

"I broke my nose. That's why my face looks so bad. It's not serious." Two nurses were busy hooking him up to various monitors. Brad turned his head on the pillow toward the young woman in pink scrubs. "Olivia, tell my wife I'm okay."

She smiled at him, then at me. "He'll be okay, as long as he follows orders. Can you make him do that?"

"I'll do my best."

"The doctor should be in soon. He's going to put a cast on that right leg. It's broken in two places." She looked at Brad. "You were lucky. They're clean breaks. They ought to mend without any complications."

I rose from the chair and stepped to the side of the bed. "How did you do this?"

"I was working on the second floor of the house. I tripped over my toolbox and fell through the stairwell. It was my own fault. I wasn't paying enough attention."

"What else is hurt?"

"Besides my ego?" His chuckle ended in a grimace.

I saw no humor in the situation. "Yes, besides your ego. Is anything else broken?"

"No, nothing else. I've got a couple of cracked ribs, a sprained shoulder, and some scrapes. That's all."

That's all?

He made it sound as if his injuries were nothing more than a minor inconvenience, but we both knew it was more than that. Much more. Fear inched its way back into my heart. What were we supposed to do now? He'd barely found a job and now this.

My knees weakened. I took a quick step backward and sat on the hard plastic chair.

Surely God had forsaken us.

Many hours later, I made up the sofa bed in the family room. This would be Brad's bedroom until he could manage the stairs again.

Because he couldn't use crutches—not with cracked ribs and a bad shoulder—he was forced to use a wheelchair to get around. He was none too happy about it. But he learned his lesson when he tried to hop his way to the downstairs bathroom. He only made it a couple of jumps before pain forced him back into the chair.

"Follow the doctor's orders," I said. "Remember?"

"Yeah, I remember." There was a sharp edge in his voice.

He'd been good natured throughout his time in the ER, joking with the nurses and doctor, making fun of how he got his injuries. But now that he was at home, cracks were beginning to show in his humor.

"Maybe I'd better help you into the bathroom."

"I can manage, Kat. You go on to bed. You look dog tired."

He might as well have told me I looked old. Well, why not? I felt old. I felt tired and old and unattractive and anxious and depressed and helpless and hopeless. And a lot more things besides.

"Good night then." I turned on my heel and headed for the stairs.

"Kat?"

I stopped and looked over my shoulder.

"I'm sorry. I didn't mean to bark at you."

I gave him a nod, then continued on my way. Once upstairs, I sank onto the twin bed in Emma's room, hid my face in my hands, and had a good cry.

Brad

HE LAY ON THE SOFA BED, HURTING FROM HEAD TO TOE, unable to sleep even after taking one of the painkillers prescribed for him at the hospital. Moonlight fell through the half-open miniblinds. If he had the strength, he would get up and close them, but he was too tired to bother.

"What now, God?" he whispered.

He'd thought things were about as bad as they could get, and then they got worse. How does a guy go lower than rock bottom? Impossible—but somehow he'd managed it.

He massaged his right shoulder with his left hand, releasing small grunts as his fingers kneaded the taut muscle.

Katherine was scared, and he couldn't blame her. Look how

he'd let her down. His reputation was in ruins. He was unemployed for the second time in less than two months. And because of his injuries, it would be weeks before he could start looking for work again. He'd only had two days on the job. What kind of benefits would he get from workers' compensation? Couldn't be much. But at least the medical expenses would be covered.

What did I do to deserve this?

As if in answer to his silent question, he thought of Nicole. He remembered the many times she'd come into his office to discuss financial matters at In Step and how easily their conversations had strayed to other things. She'd seemed to take a real interest in everything at the foundation, and he'd appreciated that about her. He'd liked bouncing ideas off of her. She'd been easy to talk to.

Perhaps too easy.

He'd been adamant in declaring himself innocent. But was he?

Twenty-seven

I AWOKE WELL BEFORE DAWN, REMNANTS OF A DREAM lingering at the edge of consciousness. An anxious dream. Even in sleep I couldn't escape my worries.

I had to find work. I had to bring in some income before we drained our savings completely. Brad wouldn't be able to work. Not for weeks. It was up to me.

The house was dark and silent as I made my way down the stairs and into the den. The computer awakened with a touch of the mouse. I sank onto the desk chair and opened the word-processing program to a new document. Trouble was I didn't know what to put on that blank page. I didn't know the first thing about creating a résumé.

You're hopeless.

I didn't have to be hopeless.

Who'd want to hire you?

I wasn't stupid. I was a fast typist. I understood computers and the Internet. I knew how to do simple bookkeeping. I was good at planning and organizing things. I knew how to delegate too. I used to help Brad all the time with In Step.

Why did I stop?

That was a dumb question. I hadn't had much choice, not once the foundation grew too large to stay in our home. I had two young daughters to care for and this house and—

I shook my head. I needed to concentrate on writing a résumé. The past was the past and couldn't be undone. Right now I needed to find a job. Any job. I opened the Web browser and googled "résumé writing." In one second, a long list of links appeared. I clicked on the first one and began to read.

I was still at the computer, wearing my silk pajamas and robe, when the doorbell rang. I expected to see darkness beyond the den's window when I looked up, but the day had arrived while I worked on my résumé. The results weren't great but had improved some.

I glanced at the clock, then got up and walked to the window, moving aside the blinds enough to see a car in the driveway.

Emma's car. Tension spread across my shoulders and along my spine. She'd been upset with me when I called her last night, angry that I hadn't let her know sooner about her dad's accident. I'd told her to come by today, but I hadn't meant before eight o'clock in the morning.

I heard her voice in the hallway. Either she'd used her key to let herself in or Brad had opened the door for her. I hoped it was the former. If the latter, Emma would have one more reason to be angry with me.

I drew a deep breath as I walked toward the door. By the time I was out of the den, Emma was in the kitchen with Brad.

"Mom didn't even call me until they were ready to release you," she said after kissing him on the cheek. As she straightened, she noticed me, and her eyes narrowed.

"Morning, Emma." I tried to sound more cheerful than I felt. "I didn't expect you to come over this early. I haven't made coffee yet."

She looked at her dad again. "I take it you haven't had breakfast either."

"No, but I—"

"I'll fix you something right now. How do waffles sound? Or I could scramble some eggs." She opened a nearby cupboard. "Or there's plenty breakfast cereal if that's what you want."

"I'd better stick with lighter fare. I'll be immobile for a while. How about a bowl of Grape-Nuts and a glass of OJ?"

Emma didn't have to ask where anything was. She'd spent most of her growing up years in this house, and I hadn't moved anything since she left home.

After the coffee was brewing, I excused myself and went upstairs to get dressed. I wasn't alone more than five minutes before there was a knock on the bedroom door.

"Come in."

Emma opened the door. Her gaze traveled around her old room. "You're still staying in here?"

"Yes."

"I thought maybe you'd've had second thoughts by now." She stepped in and closed the door behind her.

My heart sank. I wasn't up to another altercation. "Did you need something?"

She drew a breath and released it before answering. "I wondered what I can do to help take care of Dad over the next few weeks."

That wasn't the answer I expected.

"Unless the baby decides to come early, there's no reason why I couldn't come over for a while every day. Or do your grocery shopping or whatever other errands you might need."

I weighed her offer a few moments, wondering if I should accept. We hadn't been on the best of terms. Would this make things worse? Maybe, but I didn't see many other choices.

"Actually, I *could* use your help." I began brushing my hair.

"I have to find a job to tide us over until your father is back on his feet. There's no telling what sort of work I'll find to do or what hours I might have to work."

"Wow. I never imagined this would happen." Emma sat on the foot of the bed. "Are your finances that bad? I always thought you two were pretty set after Dad sold his company."

"Most of that went into In Step. But we have a little set aside."

"Dad must feel awful. I mean, you haven't worked outside the home since you two got married. That's got to wound his pride."

I didn't know if Brad would feel awful about it or not since we hadn't discussed it yet. But I knew what I felt—scared. I'd been afraid for weeks. Afraid about money. Afraid about the future. Afraid about the state of my marriage. Afraid that others— including my youngest daughter—would see how afraid I was.

"Jason said he'll take care of the yard work for Dad, so the two of you don't need to worry about that."

Unwelcome tears sprang to my eyes. My words came out gruff and not much above a whisper. "Tell him 'thank-you' for me." I was grateful, but I didn't sound like it.

"Mom?"

I set the hairbrush on the dresser as I tried to swallow the lump in my throat. I didn't want to cry again. I was tired of feeling out of control. I was tired of feeling angry one minute and depressed the next.

Emma rose from the bed, and her voice softened. "I'm sorry

for the way I talked to you on Saturday and again last night. I was wrong to say the things I did. Please forgive me."

My throat tightened again with a fresh surge of emotions, emotions that made me ashamed of myself, emotions that made me feel weak and pitiable. So unlike the person I used to be.

"I'll try to keep my opinions to myself from now on." She offered a wry smile. "It won't be easy, but I'll try." She reached for the door. "I'll go see if Dad needs anything else."

Silence swirled around me as the door closed behind Emma. Alone. So alone.

I turned to look at my reflection in the mirror and wondered if I looked as different on the outside as I felt on the inside. Would I ever get to be the old me again?

Hayley

IT WAS 11:45 A.M. WHEN SOMEONE RAPPED ON THE DOOR-jamb of Hayley's office, breaking her concentration.

"Hey there, sis."

Hayley looked up from the open file on her desk. "Emma. What are you doing here?"

"I was hoping we could go to lunch."

Hayley hadn't spoken to her sister since their fight over the telephone. She wasn't sure she was ready to see Emma yet. "I'm rather busy."

"Please."

She rolled her eyes and released a sigh. Sometimes it was easier to give in to Emma than argue with her. "All right, but it'll have to be a quick one." She opened the bottom drawer of her desk and removed her purse. "We can walk to the place on the corner."

"That's fine with me."

They were silent as they rode the elevator to the ground floor. Hayley wondered how long it would be before Emma got to the point of the visit. She was certain it had something to do with their parents.

Once they were outside on the sidewalk, Emma said, "I guess Mom called you about Dad's accident." They turned west toward the corner bistro.

"Yes. She called me last night from the hospital."

"Are you going to see him? I know he'd like you to."

Hayley waited a couple of moments before she answered, "When I can." She prepared herself for a lecture . . . but it didn't come.

"I was over there this morning to see him. He's pretty banged up and in more pain than he wants to let on. We can all thank God he wasn't hurt worse than he is."

Hayley made a noncommittal sound, letting her sister know she listened.

They reached the bistro. It was already bustling with lunch-hour customers. They moved through the line with their trays, selecting the à la carte items that appealed to them. Neither tried to continue their conversation until they were seated at a table in the courtyard.

"Hayley, I'm sorry we fought the other night."

She didn't want to apologize, but there seemed no way to avoid it. "Me too."

Emma's smile was tinged with sadness. "It's been a rough few weeks for our family."

"I believe that could be called an understatement."

"Shall we say grace?"

"Sure." She bowed her head and spoke a quick prayer, one she'd said a thousand times before.

Emma kept her head bowed a few seconds after Hayley's "amen," then looked up and smiled again. "Thanks for taking the time for this. I hate it when we argue."

Hayley loved her sister, but it was true that the two were often like oil and water. They were different in far more ways than they were the same. But bless her, Emma seemed oblivious to it most of the time.

"Mom's going to start job hunting tomorrow."

Hayley stared at her sister, wide eyed. "Mom's looking for work?"

Emma nodded as she lifted her sandwich from her plate with both hands.

"What on earth will she do? She hasn't had a job since before I was born."

"Office work of some kind, I guess. I said I'd take care of Dad whenever she's out. At least until the baby comes. By then, Dad ought to be able to manage for himself."

Hayley turned her gaze away from her sister. At a nearby

table, a little girl in a pink dress stood beside her mother, tottering on tiptoes while holding onto her mother's thigh. She jabbered in the language of toddlers, happy to entertain herself with her own nonsensical sounds.

Hayley's heart pinched with a longing so strong, it took her breath away. She'd hoped for a girl. She'd never told anyone that, not even Steve, but she'd wanted a daughter first. Now she lay awake at night, aching for the child she would never name, never know, never kiss. Sometimes the pain was so great she thought she might die from it. People had told her she would have other children. They said it, meaning to be kind, but they didn't understand that this child would still be lost to her.

Would she even have the courage to try again? She wasn't sure.

Steve said she needed to deal with her loss of the baby, that she was holding in too many emotions. Perhaps he was right. She vacillated between anger and sorrow, minute by minute, hour by hour. Except for when she succeeded in feeling nothing. She much preferred feeling nothing. It was easier to get through the day that way.

"Hayley?"

She gave her head a shake and looked at her sister again. "I'm glad you're not working so you can be there for Mom and Dad. I'm sure they appreciate it." She took the fork from its place beside her plate. "Now I'd better eat. I need to get back to the office."

Twenty-eight

I WAITED UNTIL BRAD WAS NAPPING IN THE FAMILY ROOM. Then I called Susan at her office and told her all that had happened since the last time we spoke.

"Girlfriend," she said when I finished my tale of woe, "I didn't think things could get worse for you, but they sure have."

"Thanks. I was hoping you could cheer me up."

She chuckled—and a more unrepentant sound I'd never heard.

"I'm going to start job hunting tomorrow. Maybe next time you visit Wal-Mart I'll be there to greet you."

"Ugh!"

My misery wasn't enjoying her company. "I know. But I worked and worked on my résumé this morning, and nothing I do makes it seem like I'm qualified for much else. I can do bookkeeping, but I have no formal training. I'm a fairly good typist, but I haven't been employed since the eighties and never held an office job. I haven't even volunteered at In Step in a decade. *Plus* I'm forty-five."

"You make it sound like you're at death's door. Kat, you've got a lot of life left in you. Haven't you heard fifty's the new forty?"

"I heard, but I'll bet employers don't think so. Look how hard it was for Brad to find something, even with all his experience."

She was silent so long I wondered if we'd been disconnected. "Susan?"

"I'm here. I was just thinking. What about interior decorating? I don't know anyone else who can decorate on a shoestring the way you can. The things you've done in your home are nothing short of amazing. I look at something in a secondhand store and see junk. You look at it and see possibilities. Even shopping for new furniture overwhelms me. Too many choices."

I felt a flutter of excitement but tamped it down. "Yeah, but that was for my home and the pleasure I took in doing it. That's different from it being a job. Besides, wouldn't I have to have some sort of training or business license or something if I was going to do it professionally?"

"I haven't a clue. But it seems to me that anybody can go on the Internet and claim to be an expert at one thing or another.

Why not you? There was that article in the paper awhile back about home organization and management. You must've read it. There are people whose sole job it is to go into other people's homes or offices and help them get rid of clutter and organize what they keep. And I saw a special on TV not long ago about a woman who helps stage homes for sale. You could do that blindfolded."

"You're serious, aren't you?"

Susan laughed. "Darn tootin', I'm serious. Come to think of it, I should hire you to give my place a facelift. Everything about it is so yesterday."

Whether she knew it or not, Susan had fulfilled my wish. She'd cheered me up. I didn't feel as useless as I'd felt minutes before.

"Kat"—the mirth was gone from her voice—"I'm serious. Would you let me hire you to redecorate my home?"

The excitement was back. More than a flutter this time. A whole wave of it, sweeping over me. "I wouldn't have the first notion what to charge."

"We can find that out. I'll pay you the going rate, whatever it is."

"You'd better let me think on it. And I should talk to Brad. He might not—"

"You don't need his permission. After everything that's gone on . . ." She left the sentence unfinished.

I found it odd that I'd questioned Brad's fidelity and honesty almost daily for the past month, but I didn't want others to do the same. I didn't want Susan to dismiss or belittle him. I opened my mouth to tell her so, but she spoke first.

"Listen, I've got to run. I have an appointment in ten minutes, and I'm not ready for it. I'll call you tonight after I'm home from work."

"Okay." A click on the other end of the line, followed by the dial tone.

I set the portable handset on the table and leaned back on the kitchen chair. Could I do what Susan suggested? Could I earn enough helping women get organized or decorate their homes on a budget? It could be two months, maybe three before Brad was able to work again. Could I find enough clients from the get-go?

I rose from the chair and walked from the kitchen, down the short hallway, and into the formal living room. A smile tweaked the corners of my mouth as my gaze moved around the room. It was pretty in here. The color scheme was warm and inviting, and the furniture was comfortable. In the far corner was the antique cabinet that I'd refurbished to use as a curio display. The pillows on the sofa and loveseat were some I'd quilted myself. The wall hangings had been discovered at craft fairs or in thrift shops.

Yes, it was a pretty room, but it had evolved over time. It wasn't as if I walked in here one day and said I wanted everything

to look like this. If I were to decorate someone else's home . . . A picture of Susan's living room popped into my head. It could use a makeover. If she recovered that sofa in a solid color, a beige or taupe, and then went with warm-colored accents, that room would come alive.

My smile broadened. There was no reason I couldn't help my best friend redecorate her home *and* look for another job at the same time. There would be a limited number of places where I could fill out applications or leave résumés each day. After that, time would be my own for as long as Emma was able to help care for Brad. Once she had her baby, other arrangements would have to be made. But for now . . .

I headed for the den and another lengthy session in front of the computer, this time to learn everything I could about the business of interior decorating.

My stomach growled, causing me to lift my eyes from the computer screen to the clock on the wall. I couldn't believe the time. It was almost five-thirty.

As I left the den, I heard clattering sounds coming from the kitchen. When I got there, Brad was setting a saucepan on the stovetop. A can of Campbell's vegetable beef soup was on the counter nearby.

"Brad, let me."

He looked over his shoulder. "I was about to fix myself some soup for supper. Want some?"

"You shouldn't be doing that yourself."

"I figured you were busy. Haven't seen you all afternoon." He grimaced, and pain flashed in his eyes before he straightened in his chair again.

The physician at the hospital had told us it would take time and lots of rest for the cracked ribs to heal. They couldn't be immobilized like his broken leg because doing so put a person at risk for severe lung problems. We'd been told that just breathing would hurt for a good while.

"Next time you get hungry, call me. I don't need you to make yourself worse." I moved to the back of his wheelchair and rolled him away from the stove toward a more open area of the kitchen. "Give me a few minutes, and I'll whip up something better than canned soup and crackers."

He repositioned his chair so he could see me without twisting his body. The swelling in his face was better this afternoon, but it had been replaced by two black eyes. He looked like he was the loser in a barroom brawl.

I turned around. After a short perusal inside the refrigerator and the pantry, I decided on tuna salad over lettuce and crispy chow mein noodles. I set to work at once.

"What's kept you so busy this afternoon?" Brad asked after a lengthy silence.

"You don't need his permission," Susan taunted in my memory. And she was right. I didn't need Brad's permission. Still, telling him my decision wouldn't hurt anything.

I opened a can of tuna fish and drained the water into the sink. "I was doing some research on the Internet. I'm thinking of trying my hand at interior decorating." I set the can on the counter and turned, leaning my backside against the edge of the sink. "I'm going to have to get a job of some sort. I'm not qualified for much. But Susan thinks I could help others with decorating homes and offices."

Brad didn't say a word, and with his face distorted because of his broken nose, I couldn't tell what he thought.

"Emma agreed to stay with you while I job hunt. If I'm lucky enough to find something soon, she'll come over while I'm at work. By the time she has her baby, you should be more mobile."

"Sounds like you've got it all worked out."

"Not all." I felt defensive—and didn't like it. I shouldn't feel that way.

I returned to my dinner preparations, anger stirring in my chest. Anger was somehow preferable to the host of other emotions I'd felt of late.

"You'll be a good designer, Kat. You'll be good at whatever you decide to do. I'm always amazed at what you can accomplish. You learn things twice as fast as I ever could. In Step never would have gotten off the ground without your help." He paused, then added, "I've missed your feedback since we moved the office into the Henderson Building."

His words—meant as a compliment—didn't soothe my anger. In fact, they seemed to make it worse. I pressed my lips together as I chopped bread-and-butter pickles on the countertop, then scooped them into the bowl with the tuna fish and salad dressing.

After another period of silence, Brad said, "I called Stan earlier. He's going to drop by to see me tomorrow. About ten in the morning. Will you be here?"

"Do I need to be?" I opened the cupboard and removed two plates and a couple of glasses. "I planned to go to Job Services first thing in the morning, and then, after I apply wherever they send me, I thought I'd visit a few furniture stores in town, just to get some ideas." I glanced at him. "Emma will be here."

He gave a slight shrug of his shoulders. "That's fine. You don't need to be here for Stan. He said he's got an update on In Step and the AG, but I think he's mostly coming over to see how I am."

I felt a twinge of guilt. I hadn't called anyone at church about Brad's accident. I should have. At the very least, I should have advised the prayer team or my Bible study group by e-mail. But I hated feeling needy. I didn't want people to know our business. Too much of it had become public knowledge already.

Pride. My objections revealed plain unadulterated pride on my part. There was no pretending otherwise.

I shook my head, hoping to drive away such thoughts. I had enough problems without dredging up new ones.

Twenty-nine

MY FIRST EXPERIENCE WITH JOB SERVICES LEFT ME disheartened. Even though I used some creativity when writing my résumé—volunteer work should count as experience, shouldn't it?—I got the distinct impression the job counselor deemed me a hopeless case.

It was close to noon when I entered a furniture store located near downtown Boise. I wandered through the various displays, taking note of colors and patterns and lines. I saw a number of items that would be perfect for my friend's home. And if I could convince her to spring for new carpet, the possibilities expanded.

I was sitting on a cocoa-colored sofa in a soft suedelike

material, running my hand back and forth over a seat cushion, when I heard someone say my name. I turned to see who it was. Fran Thompson. A former neighbor. A couple of years before, she and her husband had built a large new home—*mansion* was the more accurate term—in an upscale community outside of Boise. I'd lost track of her since then.

"What a surprise to find you here," Fran said as she walked toward me.

I stood. "It's been a while since we've seen each other. How are you? How's Curt?"

"We're fine." Her brows drew together in what I assumed was supposed to be a concerned frown. "The question is how are you? I feel so awful about your current troubles."

Fran and I hadn't been close friends. We'd been neighbor-hood acquaintances. Nothing more. Women who exchanged a few words when we met at the mailbox or the grocery store.

"We always thought you and Brad were such nice neighbors. Never would we have guessed you'd have to go through some-thing . . . well . . . you know. Like this. I was telling my mother when she called the other day how the things they've said in the newspaper about your husband took me so by surprise. He didn't seem the type."

The blood cooled in my veins at the same time my cheeks grew warm. There was a humming in my ears. Sounds were dis-torted, as if the piped-in music from the overhead speakers was half a turn off the right channel. I looked toward the front of the store, wishing for a straight path of escape.

"Are you moving, Katherine?"

"Moving?" My gaze returned to her. "No. Why?"

"Oh, I thought, here you are in a furniture store . . ." Translation: *I thought you must be leaving Brad, divorcing him, moving on.*

I tried to smile, tried not to show that her words had upset me. "I'm not shopping for myself. I'm getting some interior design ideas in mind to show my client." My client. That was rich.

"Really?" She lifted her perfectly waxed eyebrows. "I didn't know you were a designer."

Did my nod constitute a lie? I mean, if I did this for Susan, that made her my client and me a designer. Right? With any luck, Fran wouldn't ask for my business card.

I looked at my watch. "Oh, dear. I didn't realize the time. I'm going to be late if I don't hurry." Another forced smile. "It was good to see you, Fran. Say hello to Curt for me. I hope you're both enjoying your new home."

I didn't wait for her to respond before I made my way through the dense furniture groupings toward the front of the store. The instant I stepped through the doorway, I gulped in air, like a drowning woman breaking the surface of the ocean. I hurried toward my car, unlocking the door with the remote well before I reached it. The surge of adrenaline had my head pounding by the time I slipped behind the steering wheel, eyes closed, head bowed.

I hate this. I hate this. I hate this.

I drew in a breath and released it through my mouth. Once, then again. My pulse began to slow. After another breath, I straightened and looked about. Traffic flowed on the street beyond the parking lot, green lights turning amber, amber lights turning red, red lights turning green in timed succession. As if everything were normal and right in the world when I knew good and well it wasn't.

Seated in his wheelchair in the family room, the telephone pressed to his ear, Brad waved at me when I entered through the back door later that afternoon. I returned the wave, then looked to see what was cooking in the kitchen. I'd been so upset after my run-in with Fran that I forgot to eat lunch. Now I was ravenous. I lifted the lid on the Crock-Pot. Some sort of stew made with tomato sauce, onions, potatoes, and hamburger. Nothing fancy but it smelled delicious.

"Hi, Mom."

I turned toward Emma.

"How'd it go today?"

I shrugged. "Not great. I only filled out one application. I either lack the skills or the educational requirements for most things I'm interested in." I set my purse on the counter and slipped out of my shoes, scooting them into a corner with my big toe. "But I'm going to enjoy doing the makeover on Susan's house. I spent a couple of hours at her place this afternoon, and I've got a number of good ideas."

"That's good." Emma tipped her head toward the family room. "Dad's had a pretty good day. His ribs hurt, and his leg's starting to itch. He's talking to Pastor Mike right now."

"I won't disturb him then."

"You didn't let Pastor Mike know that Dad was hurt, did you?" Censure was back in her tone.

I opened the refrigerator and removed the pitcher of iced tea.

"You should have called him, Mom."

"I know. I . . . forgot."

Emma came to stand beside me, placing her hand lightly on my upper arm. "It isn't like you to forget stuff like that."

No, she was right about that. It wasn't like me not to do the right thing in the right way at the right time. But nothing in my life was as it was supposed to be. I wished she understood that.

I wished everyone understood it.

Emma released a soft sigh. "I'd better go home. I've got to get dinner ready for Jason. I'll be back in the morning. Is nine o'clock still okay?"

"Yes, I think that's plenty early." I took a sip of tea. "I'll go fill out any applications for job possibilities, then I'll go back to

Susan's. She's taking tomorrow afternoon off so we can make decisions about new carpet and what colors to paint the walls."

"Do you plan to be out all day? I thought you might want to be back earlier tomorrow."

I rubbed my forehead with the fingertips of my left hand. "I really don't know how long it will take, Emma. Is it important for me to tell you now?"

The silence in the room grew thick. I looked toward my daughter and found myself condemned in her eyes. Why, I couldn't say. For no good reason I could think of. After all, she'd volunteered to stay with her dad while I was working, and working was what I would be doing with Susan tomorrow.

"No," she answered. "I guess it isn't important. Not to you, anyway." She turned on her heel and strode into the family room.

"Hold on a second, Mike," I heard Brad say. Then he accepted our daughter's kiss on his cheek, thanked her for all she'd done, and told her he would see her in the morning.

Emma didn't look my way a second time as she headed for the front door. A second or two later, it closed behind her.

I didn't know what I'd done to earn another round of Emma's anger, but I was tired of it. I was tired of being judged by someone who hadn't a clue what it was like to walk in my shoes.

I went upstairs to change out of my businesswoman's job-hunting attire, replacing it with jeans and a loose-fitting top. Then with a practiced hand, I swept my hair off the back of my neck and caught it with a clip.

Would I be happier if I left him?

My heart stuttered, then began to race. I turned my gaze toward the mirror above the dresser.

Even the Bible gives me a pass if he was unfaithful.

"Do you want a pass?" I whispered.

My reflection didn't answer.

Sleepless, heartsick, I left Emma's old bedroom some time after two in the morning and walked down the hall to the master bedroom. There, I stood in the darkness, staring toward the empty bed. The bed I had long shared with my husband. Tears slipped from my eyes and made slow paths down my cheeks.

I missed Brad more than I could say. I missed the easy camaraderie we'd shared. I missed his teasing, and I missed teasing him. I missed the times I would lie in his arms, just before sleep overtook us, feeling secure and loved. I missed his warm breath on my skin as he whispered those proverbial sweet nothings in my ear. I missed the way he used to read something in the Bible and then share with me what the Lord had shown him about applying it to his own life. I missed watching old movies together, a bowl of popcorn on the sofa between us.

Sniffing, I moved toward my side of the bed. The side that

had been mine throughout our marriage. I pulled a tissue from the box on the nightstand and dried my eyes. Then I lifted the top sheet and comforter and slid into the cool softness that awaited me.

Lying on my side, I reached across to Brad's side of the bed, touching where his pillow should have been, where he should have been. When I pressed my face against the sheet and breathed in, I caught the scent of him, a whisper of his favorite cologne.

A tiny sob escaped my throat.

I didn't want to be alone. Not in this bed. Not in my life. But how could we mend all that was now broken between us? It seemed so impossible.

Thirty

I MET SUSAN FOR LUNCH AT A RESTAURANT NOT FAR FROM Lowe's, our first shopping destination.

As soon as the waitress took our orders, Susan leaned forward, arms on the table. "You don't look as excited about redecorating my place as you were yesterday. What's bothering you, girlfriend? Spill."

"Nothing new. Just the same things." I looked toward the ceiling in the far corner of the restaurant. "I can't find a job. Hayley won't take her dad's calls. Emma is angry at me for not behaving differently. Whenever we're together, Brad watches me with wounded eyes. And I don't know which way is up anymore."

Susan nodded but said nothing.

I drew in a ragged breath. "Do you think it's possible for a marriage to be repaired once trust is lost?"

"Anything's possible, Kat. But making a marriage work isn't easy in the best of circumstances. When they're not the best . . ." She shrugged.

Tears threatened, and I concentrated on forcing them back into hiding.

Susan wasn't fooled. "Listen. You want some advice?"

I nodded, but I wasn't sure it was true. Not if she said something I didn't want to hear.

"Kat, women stay with men for all kinds of reasons. Some good. Some not so good. You? I think you've stayed with Brad because of what the Bible says. Without your faith, I think you'd've hightailed it out of there long before now." She paused as the waitress delivered our drink orders, then played with the paper on her straw for a few moments before continuing. "You know what? I envy you. Maybe if I had half your faith, I'd've stayed married to Ogden and we could have made it over those bumps we had in the road of life. He wasn't a bad man, you know, or a bad husband. He was a pretty decent guy, all things considered. He loved me when I let him."

My surprise must have shown. I'd never heard Susan express regret over her divorce. Either one of them.

She waved her hand, as if trying to erase what she'd said. "Here's what I meant to say: get over yourself. Fish or cut bait."

I leaned back against the cushion of the booth.

"Be married or don't be married. Just quit being . . . uncommitted to either one. That's not fair to anybody. Not to your girls or to Brad or to yourself. Shoot, it's not even fair to your best friend." She touched her collarbone with the fingertips of one hand, as if I needed her to remind me who my best friend was. "I'll root for you and Brad to make it, or I'll root for you to make it on your own. But what you're doing now? Waffling back and forth, feeling sorry for yourself without doing what you need to change things? It's hard to root for that."

Softly, I said, "Why not tell me how you *really* feel?"

She laughed, and I managed a wry smile in return. More might have been said, but our waitress arrived with our meals. I was grateful, for by the time the girl left, I was ready to steer our conversation to carpet and wall paint and away from me.

"Tell me what's happened since you were last here," the counselor said at the beginning of our one-hour session.

As I detailed the events of the past week—my run-in with Nicole at the store, my move into Emma's old room, our children's anger, the way I'd felt in church on Sunday, Brad's accident, my job search, Susan's less than gentle words of advice over lunch—I thought of Eeyore, the gloomy blue gray donkey from Winnie the Pooh. Was I starting to sound like him?

"Everything feels so out of control." I reached for a tissue. "Susan says I'm waffling back and forth, that I'm just feeling sorry for myself. I guess she's right. I do feel sorry for myself. I want things to be as they were before all of this began."

"Katherine, have you thought about why you distrust Brad when there is no evidence against him, except for Nicole's word?"

That seemed an odd question. Of course, I had. Hadn't I?

Donna gave me a knowing smile. "We can't always alter our circumstances, and we can't control how others behave or think, no matter how hard we try. Our focus must be on what we need to change about ourselves—our attitudes, our words, our actions—even if our circumstances and the other people in our lives remain the same."

"What if I don't know what I need to change about myself?"

"Ask God to show you."

Ask God. Yes, I should do that. I should pray about it. But if God answered, I feared I wouldn't know it. There was too much noise and confusion in my head these days to hear a still, small voice.

I arrived home around three o'clock in the afternoon. Emma's car wasn't in the driveway, which surprised me. She hadn't told me she'd be leaving early. I parked my car in the garage, gathered the carpet samples and paint chips along with my purse, and headed for the back door. When I opened it, I heard music playing on the stereo.

"I'm home," I called.

No answer.

I stepped into the kitchen and dropped my things on the nearest counter. As I turned, I saw a bouquet of long-stemmed red and white roses on the table. I moved toward them. The air was thick with their sweet fragrance.

There was a small envelope in the clear plastic holder, stuck in the middle of the bouquet. It was addressed to me. I reached for it, wondering who would send me flowers and why. Then I opened the envelope and pulled out the gift card.

For the first 25 years. May we find even more happiness in the next 25. I love you. Brad.

My eyes darted from the card to the wall calendar. How was it possible I'd forgotten our anniversary? I was the one who remembered all of the milestones in my family's lives. And to forget our twenty-fifth? Impossible! And yet it was true. No wonder Emma was mad at me.

From behind me came the sound of throat clearing. I turned to face my husband.

He didn't look much like the groom I'd met at the end of the church aisle on our wedding day. Not with the skin around his eyes tinted black, purple, and yellow. Not with several days of dark stubble on his jaw.

"You're home earlier than we expected," he said. "Emma went to pick up a cake."

I glanced at the flowers. "I didn't get you anything."

"That's okay. I didn't expect you to."

That made me feel worse. "You shouldn't have spent the money."

"Maybe not. But I spent it anyway." He rolled his chair toward me. "I wanted you to know how much I love you. I wanted you to know I'll be here for you. I'll do whatever it takes, Kat, to still be your husband twenty-five years from now."

I thought of something my dad used to say when I was young: *"Katherine, today's the first day of the rest of your life. You can change your future by the choices you make today."* As a teenager, I'd thought the axiom hokey, but now I heard the wisdom behind the words.

A longing overtook me. A desire to reach out and stroke the stubble on Brad's jaw, to kiss his blackened eyes, to tell him I loved him too.

"Fish or cut bait," Susan had said. *"Be married or don't be married."*

"Ask God to show you," Donna had said about my need for change.

"You can change your future," my father had said.

What was I supposed to do now?

Emma didn't stay long after she returned from the bakery with the cake—carrot cake with sour cream frosting, "Happy 25th

Anniversary" written across it in red. She gave her dad a kiss, then gave me one too. I hadn't been sure she would.

"I'll see you both in the morning," she said on the way to the door.

A few minutes later, I went upstairs and closed myself in Emma's room. I paced from the door to the dresser to the door to the dresser. A storm of thoughts, feelings, and memories rushed through me.

Then, emotionally spent, I dropped to my knees beside the bed. "God, will You show me?"

For the longest while, I waited, strained to hear His answer. But I heard no voice. I had no vision. It seemed I was not destined to hear God the way others did.

And then, ever so slowly, there came upon me a simple moment of knowing something I hadn't known before.

Since the day of Nicole's appearance on Channel 5, I'd wanted—no, expected—God to rescue me, to make the troubles stop and go away, to restore my life to what it used to be. But here in this room, on my knees, I realized that I needed God more than I needed rescuing. I needed to draw closer to Him *in* the storm more than I needed to be taken *out* of the storm. Perhaps the realization had begun when Susan said she envied me my faith, and deep in my heart—too deep to recognize at the time—I'd feared the faith I had was too little, too whispery thin, to be envied. Was it even the size of a mustard seed?

Tears dropped onto the bedspread.

Somehow I had to find Him before I could find any of the answers I sought.

Brad

Brad had thought giving his wife flowers was a good idea. He'd thought the cake would please her. Now his confidence was shaken. He'd bungled things again. He'd failed again.

He rolled the wheelchair close to the window and gazed out at the back lawn. "What now, God? How do I fix things?"

Let go.

He stilled, waiting, listening.

Let go.

He released his breath, letting it out slowly, until he felt empty. No, not just felt it. He *was* empty.

Let her go.

That couldn't be God's voice he heard in his head and heart.

God wouldn't tell him to let Katherine go. That couldn't be how his prayers would be answered. And yet he knew it was the Lord speaking to him.

"Brad?"

His heart thudded. It hurt to breathe, and it had nothing to do with cracked ribs.

"Brad?"

He turned the wheelchair around to face the entry to the family room. There she stood, looking pale and sad. She'd been crying again.

"I . . . I need to go away for a while. A few days. Maybe a week."

Let go. Let her go. The pain in his chest intensified.

"Will you call Emma after I'm gone? I know she'll come and stay with you until I get back."

Are you coming back? The question lodged in his throat.

Her smile was brief and tentative. Then it was gone. "She'll be mad at me, but ask her to please understand this is something I need to do." She took a step closer to him. "I hope you'll understand too."

He didn't understand, couldn't understand. But when he looked into her eyes, he saw the storm in her soul, and like it or not, he knew he had to release her if she was ever to find her way back to him.

He cleared his throat, hoping his voice wouldn't crack when

he spoke. "Will you make sure someone knows where you are so we don't have to worry?"

Again that tentative smile. "I called Annabeth. She'll know how to reach me."

Her words lessened his fear.

Katherine reached out, touching his cheek with her fingertips, little more than a whisper against his skin. "I'll be back as soon as I can."

He watched as she walked toward the door that led into the garage. There, she picked up a suitcase and her purse, then glanced over her shoulder at him. One last wistful smile, and she was gone.

After the rise and fall of the garage door, Brad closed his eyes. "Whatever else happens, Father, heal her hurts. Even if it means she never comes back to me, draw her closer to You and make her heart whole again."

And so he let her go.

Thirty-one

THE CABIN NEAR PAYETTE LAKE HAD BEEN IN THE
Sorenson family for four generations. Annabeth offered it to
me the instant I told her I needed to get away for a few days.
Perhaps she could tell from the tone of my voice that there was
a storm brewing inside me.

The forest was thick with shadows by the time I pulled up
to the A-frame cabin with its cedar-shake roof and large weath-
ered deck that wrapped around two sides. When I opened the
car door, the mountain breeze brushed against my skin, the
scent of pine needles teasing my nostrils. As I released a breath,
some of the tension eased from my neck and shoulders.

I got out of the car, taking my sweater with me, and locked

it with the remote on my key chain. Then, Annabeth's written directions in hand, I followed the path across the dirt road, between two more lots, to the rough-hewn steps that led down to the lake. There was a bench at the top of the steep hillside, and I settled onto it.

Gentle waves slapped against the dock, making it rock and creak. The soft whine of a boat engine reached my ears, and I searched until I found the craft—little more than a dot moving across the water's surface—on the south end of the lake where the resort town of McCall was nestled. Somewhere behind me, a woodpecker was *ratta-tatting* a message on a tree.

But even with these sounds, the forest seemed blessedly soft and still. I breathed it in, welcoming the calm, wanting it to become a part of me.

Jesus . . . I closed my eyes. *Take control.* I drew in a deep breath.

It had seemed so important that I get away, to be alone and wait upon the Lord. I wanted to feel His presence. I wanted to hear His voice. Would He speak to me? I'd been content to read the Bible and be obedient but had never experienced what it meant to abide. I'd been content to let Him speak to others. Had I missed the chance to hear Him for myself? What was it that Jesus told the Jewish leaders? *"My sheep recognize my voice; I know them, and they follow me."* Was I among the sheep who knew the Savior's voice?

"Here I am, Lord."

I lifted my gaze to the mountain peaks, then to the clear blue sky above them. A soft wind brushed against my cheek. Overhead, the lodgepole pines swayed. Below me, the dock creaked and moaned as water lapped around its edges. But in my heart, all was silent.

Nightfall threatened before I rose from the bench and headed back to the cabin.

The first order of business was to put away the groceries I'd purchased at the market in town. Then it was time to do bit of spring housecleaning. Annabeth had warned me that no one had been to the cabin since the end of January, and the layer of dust on every surface testified to it. I found the cleaning supplies and set to work.

It felt good to expend the energy it took to clean the cabin. I vacuumed and mopped and dusted. I wiped down cupboards and countertops. I put fresh sheets on the bed in the main floor bedroom and hung clean towels in the bathroom. By the time I finished, complete darkness had settled over the forest. Silence was absolute. If anything stirred beyond the walls of that cozy cabin, I was unaware of it.

There was no television to watch—just as well—not even a DVD player for movies. But there was a boom box and a nice collection of CDs, some instrumentals but mostly worship music. I found one of my favorite performers and put the CD in the player. After adjusting the volume, I headed for the kitchen to prepare a late dinner—a grilled cheese sandwich with fresh fruit.

Half an hour later, my appetite slaked, I returned to the living room. The air had cooled sharply. It was time to try my hand at fire building. I'd never been much of a Girl Scout, but I thought I could handle this task. There was a cardboard box against the wall near the front door that was filled with old newspapers, another box with kindling, and, in a rack, enough wood to keep me warm throughout my stay.

My first few attempts were pathetic, but at last I managed to get the fire going. I took an inordinate amount of pleasure from my success as I sank onto the sofa and watched the orange flames flicking at the split logs.

For a time, I simply sat there, watching the fire, not thinking of anything, not feeling anything. Weariness tugged at my eyelids. I reached over to turn off the lamp, then lay on my side and pulled the throw from the back of the sofa over me, my gaze still on the fire in the stove.

"Hear I am, Lord. Open my ears to hear You."

I awoke with a start, a dream lingering in disjointed bits around the edge of my consciousness. I tried to remember what the dream was about, but as I sat up, it slipped away for good.

Embers glowed red inside the woodstove. I rose from the sofa, wondering what time it was, and made my way to the wood stack. After stirring the embers with the poker, I set several more logs into the stove and closed the door. In moments, the fire came to life.

Brad and I should have accepted one of the many offers from the Sorensons to use their cabin. It would have been wonderful to be up here in the mountains, surrounded by the silence of the forest, drinking hot chocolate on the deck, our feet on the railing, or snuggling together in the double bed in the downstairs bedroom. We'd often meant to, but summers had come and gone without our following through.

I walked into the kitchen and flipped the light switch. The harsh glare blinded me for a moment. After my eyes adjusted, I took the teakettle to the sink and held it under the faucet, then set it on the stove and turned the burner on high. While the water heated, I found a large mug in one of the cupboards and spooned a generous amount of hot chocolate mix into it.

My gaze lifted to the clock on the wall. A little past midnight. *I wonder if Brad's asleep.*

Turning toward the window above the small table, I brushed aside the curtain. All I could see was my own reflection in the glass and inky blackness beyond. I let the curtain fall into place.

The teakettle began to whistle, the sound so sharp it hurt

my ears. I grabbed it from the stove, opening the spout to stop the shrill noise—all the louder for the silence outside.

Moments later, a mug of steaming hot chocolate in my hand, I returned to the living room and settled once again onto the sofa. I stared at the flames licking the inside of the woodstove. Warmer air reached toward all corners of the room and drifted toward the rafters of the vaulted ceiling.

Father, I'm here. I'm alone. I'm waiting.

The fire popped and snapped. I blew across the surface of the hot chocolate, then sipped. I tried to listen. Truly I did. I hoped to hear something in my heart, something profound and life changing. All was silent.

My thoughts turned to Brad.

I remembered him as he'd been when we were young and first falling in love—Brad, a track star in his senior year, and me, a sophomore cheerleader. I suppose I fell in love with his good looks and popularity first, but there was so much more to love about him, so much more I would discover over the years. He was bright; his thirst for knowledge was never quite quenched. He'd inherited a good work ethic from his father and tenderhearted-ness from his mother, both traits I was grateful for. He loved to laugh and was a great one for playing practical jokes, especially on his two younger brothers.

I remembered how handsome he looked on our wedding day, waiting for me at the front of the church in that gray morning jacket. He was twenty-two and a new college graduate. I was twenty and, after two years as his fiancée, impatient to be his wife. I remembered the joy in his eyes as he watched my approach. I came to him dressed in white satin, and it pleased me that I deserved to wear the color of purity. We'd wrestled with desire in our years together. Often I was afraid I would lose him because I insisted we wait, fears that worsened when he entered college. But I didn't lose him. We did wait. And at last I would be his.

I remembered him as he was on the day Hayley was born. Wide-eyed, overwhelmed, overjoyed. When he held his daughter in his arms for the first time, the look of love in his eyes made me weep. And the same was true when Emma arrived two years later to the day.

I remembered the many ways he'd changed—all for the better—beginning from the day he turned over his life to God.

Perfect. Our life had been perfect . . . until Nicole.

I set aside the mug, lay down on the sofa, and wept.

Thirty-two

THE NEXT TIME I AWOKE, IT WAS MORNING. SUNLIGHT filtered through the curtains over the large living room windows.

I sat up, feeling a bit battered from sleeping so long on the less-than-comfortable couch. I tipped my head to the right, then the left, trying to work out a kink in my neck. Finally I stood. Arms overhead, I stretched, and a groan escaped me.

Maybe a shower and a change of clothes would make me feel better.

Five minutes later, I stood beneath the spray of hot water, face turned toward the showerhead, eyes squeezed tight. *Please, God. Let this be a better day.*

I'd come to the mountains to draw closer to God, to hear

from Him, to find peace in the midst of the storm. But all I'd thought about was Brad. Last night, tears spent at last, I'd drifted to sleep while remembering the day Brad rented the office in the Henderson Building. I hadn't prayed. I hadn't read my Bible. I hadn't done anything I intended to do when I left home yesterday.

And if I wasn't careful, I might start crying again.

Turning my face away from the spray of water, I squeezed some apple-scented shampoo into the palm of my hand and rubbed it into a high lather atop my head.

Brad would be eating breakfast right about now. I wondered if Emma spent the night with him. I hoped so. It would be awful if he fell while getting in or out of that wheelchair. And he was just stubborn enough to try to do something he shouldn't.

"I want you to stay involved with the foundation. You've been with me from the start. It won't be the same without you by my side." That's what Brad had said to me the day he rented the office in the Henderson building. But had I really listened to him? *Really* listened? Perhaps not. It had scared me a little, those changes he was making in our lives, selling his business, renting an office, depending upon the Lord to provide.

I rinsed the shampoo from my hair and the bath soap from my body, then turned off the water. At once, cooler air slipped around the shower curtain, so I hurried to wrap my hair in one towel and dry off with another.

For some reason, I thought of the Birches, a charming young couple—both of them mentally challenged—who'd been a recipient family of one of In Step's earlier remodels. Perhaps the sixth or seventh one that was completed. That was a few months before Brad decided to sell his construction firm.

I remembered the day he came home from work, bursting with excitement about the Birches. "Wait until you meet them, Kat. They're wonderful! Just the kind of people I want In Step to serve. The poor and the marginalized and the forgotten. Charlie works as a janitor. He's had the same job for a decade, and his boss says he's the most reliable employee he's ever had. They don't own a car because neither of them is allowed to drive. That little house in the east end that we're working on now will be perfect for them. Charlie will only have to walk two blocks to catch the bus."

It wasn't long, a month at most, before the remodeling was finished and a low-interest loan secured. Soon after, we took Charlie and Mary out for dinner to celebrate. They were just as wonderful as Brad said and so deserving of their cute one bedroom cottage.

I frowned at my reflection in the bathroom mirror. When was the last time Brad and I took a recipient family out to dinner? Several years at least. Maybe as many as five or six. But celebrations still took place. Brad made sure of that. Many of the In Step employees attended the dinners and luncheons. Contractors and bankers went at times. Occasionally donors were there, too.

Only somewhere along the way, Brad had stopped asking me to be there.

I went into the bedroom and sank onto the foot of the bed.

In those early years, I met all the families who obtained homes through the efforts of In Step. I knew their stories—the unwed mom who wanted a safe home for her child, the divorced woman piecing her life back together after beating an addiction to drugs, the mentally challenged Birches.

When had I stopped learning their stories? Had Brad stopped telling them to me—or had I stopped listening?

Brad

"DAD?" EMMA APPEARED IN THE FAMILY ROOM DOORWAY. "Mike's here." She glanced over her shoulder as the pastor stepped into view.

"Hey, Mike." Brad motioned his friend forward. "Didn't expect you to come by again this week."

"I thought maybe you could use some company." Mike sat in the easy chair.

"If you two will excuse me," Emma said, "I've got some things to do in the other room."

Brad wasn't fooled. His daughter was making herself scarce so the two men could have a private conversation. He was grateful.

He looked at Mike again. "I guess you know Katherine went away for a few days."

"Yeah. Annabeth told me."

"Do you know where she went?"

Mike gave a slight shrug at the same time he nodded.

"If it weren't for my ribs and that blasted cast, I'd be out looking for her."

"I know you would."

"And I take it you're glad I can't."

"From what little Annabeth told me, Katherine needed some time alone to work things through."

Brad released a deep sigh. "Yeah, she did. We both did." He lowered his gaze. "I've been thinking about how things got to be like this between us."

From the corner of his eye, he saw Mike lean forward in the chair, forearms braced on his thighs, ready to listen.

"Somewhere along the way, we stopped sharing certain parts of our lives. I don't think either of us realized it until now. At least I didn't."

"Why do you suppose that is?"

"I haven't figured that out yet. It's not like we weren't happy. It's not like we didn't love each other. But I must have failed her in some way or else she would have trusted me more when trouble hit. Don't you think?"

Somehow, he meant to earn back that trust.

Thirty-three

I CARRIED A LAWN CHAIR DOWN TO THE LAKE AND perched it near the end of the dock. It was warm enough for me to wear a sleeveless top and shorts, although every so often, the breeze off the water caused goose bumps to rise on my bare arms and legs.

I'd brought my Bible and a notebook with me, just in case, but I'd ceased trying to control the direction of my thoughts. I let them go where they willed. I seemed to be on some sort of mental and emotional treasure hunt, scrounging for clues that would lead me to my final destination.

I'd learned something about myself while sorting through old memories, and it wasn't very flattering. I was more concerned with appearances than I should be. I was more concerned that I *look* spiritual than that I truly *be* spiritual. How could I change that? I'd been a Christian all of my life. I'd thought I was a good one. Why hadn't I wanted to know Him more? Why had I settled for less than He wanted to give?

"Come with me, Kat."

The words floated into my mind like a piece of driftwood carried on the currents. They caught my attention and wouldn't let go.

"Come with me, Kat."

At first, it was Brad's voice I heard. He wanted me to come with him to look at the repossessed houses In Step might buy. He wanted me to come with him to see the homes as they were remodeled and restored. He wanted me to come with him when he handed the keys to the new owners.

Come with me, Beloved.

This time, the words came not from the past but from the present, from a deep, secret place inside my heart. My breath caught in my chest. I felt a warm breeze circle me, enfold me. And I *knew*. Somehow I knew. It was the Lord, touching me with those words.

Come with Me, Beloved. Trust Me.

I imagined myself standing on the edge of the dock, arms stretched out at my sides, eyes closed. I pictured myself falling backward and knowing I would be caught before I hit the water.

When was the last time I'd trusted anyone so completely? Had I ever?

"I'll trust You, Lord, if You'll help me. Starting today, I'll trust You."

It was the Friday of Memorial Day weekend, and the forest was alive with the sounds of families ready to celebrate the unofficial beginning of summer. They began arriving in the early afternoon and continued throughout the evening. Car doors slammed. Parents called to children. Children shouted to their dogs. Dogs barked as they chased after squirrels and chipmunks.

Wrapped in a comforter, I sat on the deck until after nightfall. Through the trees, I saw lights come on as my newly arrived next-door neighbors settled in. I imagined the wife dusting, sweeping, and wiping down countertops, much as I'd done the night before. But she wasn't alone. Her husband was with her. Maybe her children too.

I missed them, my family—Hayley and Emma and Brad. Hayley, too much like me, concerned with appearances, careful to keep her emotions in check. Emma, full of compassion, passionate for God, and prone to wearing her heart on her sleeve. And Brad . . .

"Oh, God, I want our marriage to be what You want a marriage to be. Will You teach me to trust?"

I lifted my gaze, up past the tall, swaying pine trees to the star-studded heavens beyond. So vast. So surprising. What had I read? That there was a star out there in the universe that was larger than earth's orbit around the sun. Something like a hundred million miles in diameter. A star we would never explore but could only look at from afar. A star among countless other stars, more than all the sand on all the beaches in the world.

All that, God had breathed into existence.

And yet He thought of me. He thought of me and saw me and cared for me and was with me. I'd prided myself on living for Him, but I never let Him in. Not really. I'd wanted Jesus as Savior but never let Him be more—Maker, Master, Father, Friend.

"Thank You, Lord, for catching me when I fall. Come in and change me."

Thirty-four

I WAS WASHING THE BREAKFAST DISHES THE FOLLOWING morning when Brad called, his distinctive ring on my cell phone causing me to stop and stare at the device, which I'd put on the kitchen table earlier.

Should I answer it or not? At first I thought that whatever he had to say, it could wait a few more hours. There was so much we needed to talk about. Too much to say over the phone. And yet . . .

I dried my hands on a dish towel as I stepped closer to the table. The phone stopped ringing. I lifted it, flipped it open, closed it again.

In the distance came the sound of hammering. Someone

getting an early start on repairs to their summer home. It was impossible to judge how far away they might be. Sounds carried a long distance in the forest.

The phone rang a second time. Still Brad.

This time I didn't hesitate. "Hello."

"Hi, Kat."

The sound of his voice made me smile.

"Sorry to call you. I know you wanted time away from me so you could think."

Not time away from you. Not really. Oh, Brad, there were so many reasons for me to get away, but escaping you wasn't one of them. I know that now.

"I need to ask for your permission for something I want to do."

"My permission?"

"I want to have Emma drive me over to Nicole's. There's something I need to say to her."

My stomach dropped. I sat on the nearby chair.

"Kat, it's complicated, but will you trust me? There are things I need to say to her. Something I have to ask her."

Trust. Wasn't that what God had called me to do? Trust Him. And if I trusted Him, then couldn't I also trust Brad?

"I promise that I have good reasons, Kat. But I won't go if you say no."

I drew a deep breath, held it, released it. "Yes."

"Yes?"

"Yes, I'll trust you." I didn't know where the strength came from to say those words.

"Thanks," he said softly. "When you get back, we'll talk about this."

"Yes."

"I hope you'll be home soon, Kat."

"I will be. Soon."

Both of us were silent for several seconds. Then he said, "I love you."

I know.

"Take care of yourself."

"I will."

Again the protracted silence. I lowered the phone from my ear and closed it, breaking the connection.

Nicole

NICOLE WAS PUTTING THE FINISHING TOUCHES ON HER sister's birthday cake when the doorbell rang. She glanced at the clock on the kitchen wall. That couldn't be Claire this soon. She wasn't due for another hour.

She wiped her hands on the dishcloth before heading for the front door. When she opened it, her heart seemed to stop beating.

There was Brad, in a wheelchair with a cast on his leg. Behind him was one of his daughters. The younger one, she thought. Brad was here, at her home. He'd come to see her. She'd succeeded at last.

Nicole had played this scene in her mind a thousand times.

She'd imagined him, defeated and destroyed. She'd pictured herself, exultant in victory, glad that she'd had her revenge. She'd envisioned many things about the moment she would see him again, but never that he would be in a wheelchair when it happened.

"Brad."

"Hello, Nicole."

She cleared her throat. "What happened to you?"

"I was in an accident."

"I guessed that much." She opened the door a little wider. "Do you want to come in?"

"No. I think it's better that I stay out here. In plain view."

She didn't care for the way his words made her feel. But if he thought she would issue any sort of retraction, he was mistaken. It wasn't in her to back down. Not ever.

Brad glanced over his shoulder. His daughter looked at him for a few moments, then nodded, turned, and walked back to his car that waited at the curb.

"What is it you want, Brad?"

He looked at her, and her heart quickened. That's the reaction she'd had around him from their first meeting. There was something about him that made him seem unlike any other man she'd known. There was something about him—in his eyes, in his smile, in the tone of his voice—that drew her to him. It always had. If only . . .

"I came to ask your forgiveness," he said.

He'd surprised her again. "*My* forgiveness?"

"Yes."

Crossing her arms, she leaned a hip against the doorjamb and tossed him a saucy grin. "And here I thought you'd be telling me *I* needed forgiveness from you or Katherine or God."

There was something in the look he gave her—patience, peace, understanding, something—that made her grin fade.

"Nicole, I've had plenty of time to think things over and pray about everything that's happened, and I realized that I was unfair to you. I thought of us as good friends and dedicated coworkers, but I see now that I crossed a line somewhere along the way. I never meant to, but I did. I'm sorry because my actions gave you the wrong impression. And that must have hurt you."

She'd expected him to bring up what she'd told the media— an affair, promises made and broken, mismanagement of charitable funds. She'd expected him to threaten her with legal actions of some sort. But he didn't. Not a word of accusation from him. What was wrong with him? He should be hurting or furious or both. Instead he watched her with . . . What? Compassion? Pity?

So help her, if he felt sorry for her, she'd slap him from here into next week.

"I apologize for anything I did or said that made you think I felt anything beyond friendship. In the future, I will be more guarded, but that doesn't undo the past. Will you forgive me?"

She'd called Katherine a fool for staying with Brad. Maybe she was wrong about that. Maybe Katherine was smarter than Nicole had believed.

Apparently accepting her silence as an answer, Brad nodded. "Thanks for at least listening."

Still without a word of accusation or condemnation, he turned the wheelchair around and rolled it down the walk. His daughter came toward him and pushed the chair the remaining distance to the car.

Nicole remained in the doorway until passenger, his wheelchair, and the driver were in the automobile. Only then did she take a step backward and close the door.

Thirty-five

I SPENT ANOTHER EVENING AT THE CABIN, STARING into the fire in the woodstove, another evening with my thoughts sifting through memories. I felt like there was so much more I needed to understand about myself, so much more God needed to reveal to me, before I could begin building a new life. A new life with God. A new life with Brad.

The apostle Paul wrote that he'd learned to be content in whatever circumstances he was in. I used to think I was content, but now I could see that my contentment was based upon how well I controlled the circumstances of my life, not upon my trust in a loving God.

How many times had I sung those words in church—God

is in control—without them becoming a reality in my heart? Susan had challenged me on that very thing. She'd told me I was fooling myself if I thought I was in control, and still I hadn't seen the truth, not even as I professed that it was God who ruled. Head knowledge but not heart knowledge. That's what my dad had called it.

The memory of my father brought a sad smile to my lips. He'd been gone almost thirty years, and I missed him still. When I was a kid, it had seemed to me there wasn't anything my dad couldn't fix. If he'd lived longer, could he have fixed me?

I lay down on the sofa, pulling the blanket over me. Shadows and firelight danced across the rafters of the vaulted ceiling.

Maybe my need to control things had begun with the death of my father. That first year after we lost him had been difficult. My world had seemed so insecure and frightening. Was that when I stopped trusting God to look out for me?

I closed my eyes, remembering how Brad had been there for me as I mourned my loss. A freshman in college with a part-time job, he'd come over as often as he could to be with me, to hold me, to let me cry on his shoulder.

Even then he was someone I could count on.

And yet I hadn't trusted him completely. I'd been afraid I would lose him too. Maybe I'd never gotten over that fear. Maybe that's why I'd worked so hard to make everything perfect, to make myself perfect so that I could control the outcome.

Only I wasn't perfect. I didn't have it all together. I'd never had control.

One more time I pictured myself, arms outstretched, falling backward, trusting that I would be captured in arms of love. And with that image in mind, I drifted into a peaceful, dreamless sleep.

Thirty-six

I CAME DOWN FROM THE MOUNTAIN ON SUNDAY AFTER-
noon. It wasn't easy to leave the Sorenson cabin or the peaceful-
ness of the forest. I felt as if I had just begun to learn the things
God wanted me to understand. What if I couldn't hear Him
anymore once I reached the valley?

But that, too, was an issue of trust. I had to trust God to
speak to me, to teach me to listen, to guide me in every way.

When I entered the house two hours later, I heard the television playing in the family room. It sounded like a sports program
of some kind. Apparently neither Emma nor Brad had heard the
garage door open, for no one called out a greeting.

Nerves fluttered in my stomach as I moved toward the family

room entrance. In some ways, it felt as if I'd been gone for months instead of days.

The sofa bed came into view. Brad was lying on top of the sheets and blanket, his back and leg propped with pillows. His eyes were closed, and when he breathed out, his lips pursed in a soundless snore.

Love welled in my heart.

Another step forward brought Emma into view. She sat in the easy chair, one arm cradling her belly, her head tipped to one side. She, too, slept.

I swallowed the lump that rose in my throat as I walked across the room to the sofa bed, leaned down, and pressed my lips to Brad's cheek. His eyes opened.

"You're home," he said.

"I'm home."

"To stay?"

I smiled. "To stay."

I heard a soft moan behind me and turned in time to see Emma finishing a stretch, arms above her head.

"Mom," she said when she opened her eyes, surprise in her voice. "When did you get here?"

"Just now. I haven't even taken my suitcase upstairs."

She stood. "How are you?" There was a host of questions packed into those three little words.

"I'm better." I nodded. "I'm good."

Whatever else Emma wanted to know, she didn't press for answers. She had wisdom beyond her years, this youngest daughter of mine. "I'll get my things and go home. Jason will be glad to have me back. He's been babysitting the puppy he gave me for Mother's Day." She winked at her father. "I definitely had it easier here."

I'd made many mistakes, I was sure, but I must have done a few things right to have raised this child to be the woman she was.

"Thank you, Emma," I said, lightly touching her shoulder.

She studied me with her eyes, looking for something, though I knew not what. But whatever it was, she must have found it, for she smiled. "I'm glad you're back." She gave me a quick hug.

"Me too."

"Call me if you need me."

I nodded. "I will."

"Bye, Dad." She leaned over to kiss him, then left the room. A short while later, the front door closed behind her.

We were alone.

I sat on the side of the sofa bed, wondering what I should say. How could I begin to tell Brad what I had learned, what I was still learning, about myself?

As if reading my mind, he asked, "Do you feel like talking?"

I twisted to look at him. "I'm not sure what to say." I touched my fingertips to my forehead. "It's still kind of confused in here."

He nodded in response, then maneuvered himself—accompanied by groans and grimaces—to the edge of the bed. Once he was seated upright beside me, he reached over and took hold of my hand. "We'll get through this."

I believed him. For the first time in weeks, I believed we would make it through. Not simply staying together for the sake of appearances, not simply enduring a marriage that was broken, but knowing we would get better, grow closer, come out stronger on the other side.

Because we trusted in a God who first loved us.

Part Three
NEW LIFE

Thirty-seven

SEVERAL MILLENNIA AGO, THE PSALMIST WROTE: I WILL *lie down in peace and sleep, for you alone, O LORD, will keep me safe.* In the weeks following my return from McCall, that's how I slept. In peace. With trust. How much better than the many restless nights when fear troubled my thoughts.

But perhaps those nights had also been of God, for the psalmist once wrote: "You don't let me sleep. I am too distressed even to pray!"

I awakened slowly on the morning of the fourth of July. The sun was up, the room brightened by light coming through the blinds. A look at the clock told me it was almost eight o'clock.

"About time you woke up." Brad stood in the bedroom

doorway, dressed in an Hawaiian shirt and khaki shorts. The skin on his right leg was pale compared to the tanned left leg, evidence of the cast he'd worn until two days ago.

I scooted up against the head of the bed, shoving my hair away from my face with one hand. "How long have you been up?"

"A couple hours. I decided to clean the grill before it got too hot out."

I should have been up early too. I had lots of cooking to do before people started arriving this afternoon. In addition to the girls and their husbands, Mike and Annabeth Sorenson, Stan and Judy Ludwig, and Susan and her date were joining us for an old-fashioned Fourth of July celebration, complete with hamburgers and hot dogs, chips, several kinds of salad, and much, much more.

But I didn't rush to rise. I was learning—step by step, moment by moment—that the world would not fall off its axis if I didn't make everything perfect, if I didn't have it all under control. My counseling sessions with Donna O'Keefe had helped a lot with those less-than-wonderful personality traits of mine.

"Want your coffee in bed?" Brad asked.

"Sure." I grinned. "But only because I know how important it is that you exercise that leg."

"Yeah, right." He smiled too. "Be back in a jiff."

I closed my eyes again, a sigh escaping my lips. *Good morning, God. Thank You for this new day.*

I had many reasons to be thankful—for the couple who had hired me last week to redesign their home's interior, for the positive conclusion of the attorney general's investigation into In Step's financial practices, and for the phone call Brad received from the president of the foundation's board of directors, reinstating him at full salary as soon as he was ready to return. But mostly I was thankful for what the Lord was doing in me, in Brad, in our marriage, and in our children.

I pictured each member of my family, one by one, and said a prayer for them.

I prayed for Hayley who'd begun tentative steps toward reconciliation with her father and with me, and peace over the loss of her child. I rejoiced that God was healing hurts I never knew she had. I prayed that she and Steve might not make the mistakes in their marriage that I'd made in mine. I prayed that they would come to put God first in their hearts.

I prayed for Emma and Jason, that God would give her a safe delivery and that their child would be healthy. I asked God to stretch their finances and to bless them for their giving hearts.

I prayed for Brad's parents and my mom. I asked God to keep them strong in their later years and to watch over them since they lived so far from us. I prayed for relationships to be mended and for generational curses to be broken.

And I prayed for Brad—because he wasn't perfect either and I'd never had the right to expect him to be.

The telephone rang. Why did people think it was okay to call before ten o'clock in the morning? Especially on a holiday.

"Can you get that, Kat? I'm on the stairs with our coffee."

I reached for the phone on the nightstand. "Hello."

"Mom!" Hayley said, excitement in her voice. "Emma's at the hospital. Jason said he thinks the baby's coming fast."

"Calm down, honey. First babies almost always take a while."

"All I know is Jason said we better hurry if we want to get there before the baby does."

"Who is it?" Brad asked from the doorway.

I held up an index finger to silence him. "I'll get dressed and we're on our way," I told Hayley. "See you there."

Brad brought the mug of coffee toward me. "See who where?"

"Emma's at the hospital. It appears our first grandchild wants to be an Independence Day baby."

I must confess, there was a moment, not many hours later, when I looked at Daniel Bradford Myers—a healthy, hearty eight pounds, with a good set of lungs—and thought, *he's perfect.*

Perhaps, in this case, I wasn't wrong to think so. For surely, every good and perfect gift came to us from God above, as had this new life, wriggling and wailing in his grandfather's arms.

A Note from the Author

Dear Friend:

I hope you enjoyed your time spent with Katherine and the family and friends who peopled her world. I love to tell stories of imperfect people in need of a perfect God—perhaps because that is an accurate description of me. No matter how many years I've walked with the Lord, there is always something new He reveals to me, something new He wants to change in me.

I'm very pleased that *The Perfect Life* is a Women of Faith novel, and I hope it will touch many hearts. Life can be hard, but for those who trust in a merciful, loving God, it is never hopeless.

On a personal note, God used a Women of Faith Conference to end a season of grieving in my life and to begin making my heart whole again. He spoke to me through the examples of the women on the stage who shared stories of life's hurts and God's faithfulness. He spoke to me through the worship times when I was surrounded by fifteen thousand other women, voices and hands lifted in praise. He spoke to me in the laughter and in the tears.

If you have the opportunity to attend a Women of Faith Conference, don't pass it by. You'll be blessed by the experience.

In the grip of His grace,
Robin Lee Hatcher
From her heart . . . to yours!
www.robinleehatcher.com

Acknowledgments

MANY THANKS FOR THE PATIENCE, GUIDANCE, AND HARD work of my wonderful editors at Thomas Nelson, Ami and Leslie. I'm delighted you not only saw the story I hoped to create at the start, but helped me to make it a reality.

Reading Group Guide

1. *The Perfect Life.* Would you be able to use this title for your own life? Why or why not?

2. With trouble brewing in the early pages of the book, Brad immediately prayed for wisdom. Things only got worse. Does that mean you might as well save your breath and wait for the outcome? Or were his prayers eventually answered?

3. In chapter 4 we discover that Katherine and Brad were married in an unequally yoked situation. Brad did become a Christian later on. How do we reconcile this with the admonition to not be unequally yoked? Have you ever been in a similar situation?

4. Hayley had a rather cynical outlook on Christian marriage, spousal faithfulness, and life in general. What might you imagine brought her to this state? Discuss ways to develop a more Christ-like attitude.

5. Katherine's friend Susan recommended cheesecake and lots of chocolate as an antidote to the growing troubles in her life. What other indulgences do we reach for to relieve life's stresses? What might be some better antidotes?

6. As their situation worsened, Kat asked, "God, why are You letting this happen?" while Brad prayed for wisdom. When Brad resigned from the Foundation to help it stay afloat, Kat said, "But it's your ministry." Brad answered, "It's God's ministry, Kat, not mine." Who is the more mature Christian? Why? How would you react in a similar situation?

7. Kat noted the differences between Emma's exuberant prayer life and her own more reserved one: "There wasn't anything formal or poetic about the words she used when talking to God." Do you think one way of praying is right, the other wrong? Or is there a time for both? What sort of prayer life do you yourself have?

8. Katherine worked hard to make her home perfect—a reflection of their marriage, family, and successful life. Why do you think this outward show was so important to her? Is that a good thing? Bad? How do you balance this in your own life?

9. Brad felt he had to confess to Kat that Nicole had unexpectedly kissed him once. This shook Katherine's trust in her husband. Should he have told her? Did she miss something in the telling—the fact that he wanted to be honest with her and counted on her trust in him—or was she right in her reaction?

10. Haley noted the public image of a saint with feet of clay was not only a popular one with the media, but also possibly a true one of her dad. Are she and today's media too quick to judge our religious leaders? What about you?

11. *"Where are You, God?* No sound. No touch. No sense of peace. Only turmoil. Only aloneness." Have you been there? What did you do?

12. Emma understands that parents may not always be perfect but they're worthy of trust and love. Hayley obviously struggled with this. What is your own relationship with your parents like? Was there ever a time when you doubted them? If so, how did that make you feel?

13. "Be careful what river you go down because I'm in the boat with you." This quote hit home with Katherine as she felt her marital lifeboat swamp. Do you think this common way of seeing a couple as one is fair? Should you—will you—be more careful about judging other couples as a unit?

14. "I did my best to walk in obedience according to the Scripture . . . That should be enough. Shouldn't it? I thought of the way Brad looked sometimes after a period of worship or following his prayer time. A look of joy that spoke of something beyond my reach." What do you think was missing for Katherine? Do you relate to this?

15. After Hayley's miscarriage, with the integrity of the Foundation questioned and the matter of fidelity raised, Katherine thought of the story of Job. How does one find a way to praise God in bad times as well as in good times? Have you had such an experience? Explain.

16. Although not tempted himself, Brad thought he could now understand why some people resort to suicide. How can we prepare ourselves ahead of time so that suicide is never a temptation when life seems broken beyond repair and our strength is used up?

17. Katherine said divorce isn't supposed to happen to people like her. She had been as good a wife as anyone could be and she was not going to have people thinking she was a failure. Nor was she going to have God thinking that of her. How is this way of thinking flawed? Do you think this is a good reason for not getting a divorce? Is there ever a good reason?

18. Katherine thought perhaps God had spared her any testing before because He knew how utterly she would fail. And wasn't her failing marriage enough without a failing faith as well? What would be a more optimistic, hopeful, godly way for Katherine to look at things? Have you felt like this?

19. Sometimes, events from our past have more effect on our lives than we realized. What did Katherine come to understand about the death of her father when she was a teenager? As far as trusting God to take care of her? As far as needing to be in control of everything? Can you share an example of this from your own life?

20. "Come with Me." Katherine heard these words and answered, finally, with abandonment of her own control, giving God her complete trust. So many of us allow Jesus to be our Savior but never get as far as letting Him also be our Master, Father, Friend. What profound changes did this new knowledge make in Katherine's life? What about your?

WOMEN OF FAITH®

Women of Faith, North America's largest women's conference, is an experience like no other. Thousands of women — all ages, sizes, and backgrounds — come together in arenas for a weekend of love and laughter, stories and encouragement, drama, music, and more. The message is simple. The result is life-changing.

What this conference did for me was to show me how to celebrate being a woman, mother, daughter, grandmother, sister or friend.
— Anne, Corona, CA

I appreciate how genuine each speaker was and that they were open and honest about stories in their life   even the difficult ones.
— Amy, Fort Worth, TX

GO, you MUST go. The Women of Faith team is wonderful, uplifting, funny, blessed. Don t miss out on a chance to have your life changed by this incredible experience.
— Susan, Hartford, CT

WOMEN OF FAITH

Novels

A Time to Dance,
KAREN KINGBURY

A Time to Embrace,
KAREN KINGSBURY

Sand Pebbles,
PATRICIA HICKMAN

The Covenant Child,
TERRI BLACKSTOCK

Gardenias for Breakfast,
ROBIN JONES GUNN

A Song I Knew by Heart,
BRET LOTT

Alaska Twilight,
COLLEEN COBLE

My Life as a Doormat,
RENE GUTTERIDGE

The Note,
ANGELA HUNT

The Pearl,
ANGELA HUNT

The Debt,
ANGELA HUNT

Stranded in Paradise,
LORI COPELAND

Reconstructing Natalie,
LAURA JENSEN WALKER
(*2006 NOVEL OF THE YEAR)

RV There Yet?,
DIANN HUNT

Quaker Summer,
LISA SAMSON
(*2007 NOVEL OF THE YEAR)

The Angels of Morgan Hill,
DONNA VANLIERE

Midnight Sea,
COLLEEN COBLE

The Wedding Machine,
BETH WEBB HART

The Perfect Life,
ROBIN LEE HATCHER

The Yada Yada Prayer Group
(*2008 NOVEL OF THE YEAR)